SEDUCED IN INK - SPECIAL EDITION

A MONTGOMERY INK: BOULDER NOVEL

CARRIE ANN RYAN

SEDUCED IN INK

A Montgomery Ink: Colorado Boulder Novel

By

Carrie Ann Ryan

Seduced in Ink
A Montgomery Ink: Boulder Novel
By: Carrie Ann Ryan
© 2020 Carrie Ann Ryan

This book is a work of fiction. Names, characters, places, and incidents either are products of the author's imagination or are used fictitiously. Any resemblance to actual events, locales or persons, living or dead, is entirely coincidental.
No part of this book can be reproduced in any form or by electronic or mechanical means including information storage and retrieval systems, without the express written permission of the author. The only exception is by a reviewer who may quote short excerpts in a review.

All content warnings are listed on the book page for this book on my website.

NO AI TRAINING: Without in any way limiting the author's [and publisher's] exclusive rights under copyright, any use of this publication to "train" generative artificial intelligence (AI) technologies to generate text is expressly prohibited. The author reserves all rights to license uses of this work for generative AI training and development of machine learning language models.

PRAISE FOR CARRIE ANN RYAN

"Count on Carrie Ann Ryan for emotional, sexy, character driven stories that capture your heart!" – Carly Phillips, NY Times bestselling author

"Carrie Ann Ryan's romances are my newest addiction! The emotion in her books captures me from the very beginning. The hope and healing hold me close until the end. These love stories will simply sweep you away." ~ NYT Bestselling Author Deveny Perry

"Carrie Ann Ryan writes the perfect balance of sweet and heat ensuring every story feeds the soul." - Audrey Carlan, #1 New York Times Bestselling Author

"Carrie Ann Ryan never fails to draw readers in with passion, raw sensuality, and characters that pop off the page. Any book by Carrie Ann is an absolute treat." – New York Times Bestselling Author J. Kenner

"Carrie Ann Ryan knows how to pull your heartstrings and make your pulse pound! Her wonderful Redwood Pack series will draw you in and keep you reading long into the night. I can't wait to see what comes next with the new generation, the Talons. Keep them coming, Carrie Ann!" –Lara Adrian, New York Times bestselling author of CRAVE THE NIGHT

"With snarky humor, sizzling love scenes, and brilliant, imaginative worldbuilding, The Dante's Circle series reads as if Carrie Ann Ryan peeked at my personal wish list!" – NYT Bestselling Author, Larissa Ione

"Carrie Ann Ryan writes sexy shifters in a world full of passionate happily-ever-afters." – *New York Times* Bestselling Author Vivian Arend

"Carrie Ann's books are sexy with characters you can't help but love from page one. They are heat and heart blended to perfection." *New York Times* Bestselling Author Jayne Rylon

Carrie Ann Ryan's books are wickedly funny and deliciously hot, with plenty of twists to keep you guessing. They'll keep you up all night!" USA Today Bestselling Author Cari Quinn

"Once again, Carrie Ann Ryan knocks the Dante's Circle series out of the park. The queen of hot, sexy, enthralling paranormal romance, Carrie Ann is an author not to miss!" *New York Times* bestselling Author Marie Harte

To my readers.

Thank you for being you.

ACKNOWLEDGMENTS

This book was so much fun. I don't always get to say that with books, but this was one a blast. I write romance because I love the idea of hope in the darkness. Where you know there will be an HEA by the end, but it's how the characters change and find their way that makes the true story.

Madison and Aaron went through SO much to get where they are and I truly hope you love this romance.

Thank you to my team for helping me make this book shine. Thank you to my girls for helping me remember it' okay to want love and hope when the darkness of the world threaten to break through.

And thank you dear readers for being part of the Montgomerys.

Happy reading, everyone!

~Carrie Ann

SEDUCED IN INK

The Montgomery Ink: Boulder series concludes with a fake relationship where the heat and emotional connection are anything but false.

The moment Madison McClard's parents tell her that her ex is getting married, there's no getting out of their latest scheme. One moment she's trying to get out of their clutches. The next, they're telling her exactly who she'll marry to save the family name. The one thing her parents don't count on, however: Aaron Montgomery.

Aaron Montgomery didn't mean to lie. Still, as soon as he overheard Madison's dilemma, the words fell out of his mouth. Now, he's fake engaged to a woman he barely knows, who also happens to be his new brother-in-law's cousin.

As the deception mounts, so does the attraction. They told themselves it was only a ruse, but as feelings ramp and dangers surge, this Montgomery may have just met his match.

He simply has to fight to keep her.

CHAPTER ONE

Madison McClard desperately wanted cheese.

She wasn't exactly sure why she craved cheese at the moment. It had never been her favorite thing before she started hanging out with her cousins-in-law.

However, because of their cheese obsession—and it was indeed an obsession—just the idea of not being able to eat cheese meant she wanted it even more.

While cheese surrounded her, little platters held by waiters in stiff white shirts and black pants with creases—almost as if they knew she wanted cheese— she could not indulge.

And she hated it.

She wasn't lactose intolerant. And she wasn't on a

diet or afraid of the food. She loved dairy and had a cheese collection of her own, along with the boards and utensils to make a perfect spread.

However, she did not want to get into a fight with her family at her cousin Lincoln's art show. That meant she would refrain from the lovely array of cheeses, crackers, and red wine that beckoned her to the dark side.

"You know you can just take a bite," her friend Aaron said from her side. She shook her head.

"I'm not taking a bite," she whispered, keeping a pleasant smile as people walked past, expectant looks on their faces. They knew she was family to the famous artist and wanted to know more about her. But she had no idea why. It wasn't as if she had any talents when it came to art, though she could decorate a mean cupcake.

"Here, let me just get you some. There's a little bit of honey on this brie, as well as an apple slice that makes the perfect crisp crunch when you bite into it."

She turned her gaze towards Aaron and studied his face. He might be sexy as hell with that tousled brown hair, those blue eyes, and his chiseled jaw, but she wanted to smack him.

He was far too handsome and charming for his own good.

"I'm not indulging. And how did you even know I wanted cheese? You're not a mind reader, are you?"

He smiled, flashing perfectly white teeth, a little dimple in his cheek poking out.

A dimple? How the hell had she not noticed that before?

Damn him and that stupid divot.

And that bitable jaw.

And lickable neck.

Where the heck had those thoughts come from?

"I saw you practically drooling over a platter, your hand outstretched for a bare instant before you let it drop casually as if no one would notice."

She looked down askance at her hands, then back up at Aaron. "I did not."

Aaron snorted. "Okay, the hand thing was an exaggeration. But you did gaze longingly."

Madison winced. "I hope no one else saw me looking like that." Namely, her mother.

"I don't think so. But, for all I know, everybody knows your love of cheese."

She resisted the urge to flip him off and then moved closer to him. The heat of him seared her side when someone brushed past, ironically holding a full plate of cheese.

"You're drooling again," Aaron said, wrapping his

arm around her waist. He gave her hip a squeeze before moving back. It was a friendly touch, nothing flirty, just someone trying not to fall as they both moved out of the way.

It still made her heart race, and she had no idea why.

She did not have a crush on Aaron Montgomery. He was her cousin's love's brother, and things got far too complicated with all of those connections. Considering that her cousin was with Aaron's brother Ethan, as well as Holland, things were a little complicated already, and she wanted no part of adding to that.

And it didn't really matter because Aaron moved away, still smiling at her but in a friendly way, maybe even brotherly.

Just because he was handsome as hell didn't mean she needed any part of that. She could look, but no way would she ever touch.

"What do you think of all this art?" Aaron asked.

"It's stunning. And I'm not just saying that because Lincoln is family."

Aaron nodded, looking around, his gaze that of an artist and not just an average viewer.

"Lincoln's amazing. And while he might be my family now too, I can still go on and on about his talents. I'm a little jealous, honestly."

Madison shook her head. "I've seen your art, as well."

"I play with glass most days. Lincoln breathes life into his work."

That made Madison snort, and she winced as one of her parents' friends gave her an admonishing look before walking past. Great, her parents would find out about her lack of social decorum in about ten seconds.

"You literally breathe life into your art," she said, going back to the conversation. "You're a glassblower."

He stared at her then as if looking at her for the first time. Or maybe she was seeing things. "Maybe, but I still have a ways to go until I'm happy with what I do."

"You and Lincoln should do a show together someday. And then have Bristol play her cello while in the room. Ethan can organize it all and make it a *thing*."

"I'm pretty sure I cannot afford my sister's prices," Aaron said with a wink before taking a sip of his champagne.

Madison held a glass of water, in a very fancy flute, but it was still only water.

After all, she didn't want to add any more ammunition to her parents' barbs, and she already knew those would be coming.

She hated that she never stood up to them. She might do her best most days, but nine times out of ten, she tried not to draw attention to herself so she could avoid the inevitable fight.

Lincoln wasn't a fan of the way she dealt with her parents, but he was lucky. While his parents might not always be in the picture these days because they had moved away, they weren't passively-aggressively evil like hers.

"At least you have some form of talent," Madison said wryly.

"Some form, huh? Well, at least I know where I stand."

She rolled her eyes. "I was just telling you that you're brilliant, and now that I'm trying to downplay it because you got all blushy, you think I'm making fun of you."

"I did not get all blushy," Aaron said, practically gasping.

"You could be clutching your pearls right now, and I wouldn't be surprised."

"You're a cruel, cruel woman, Madison McClard."

"So I hear," she mumbled.

Aaron frowned. "So you hear what? Who do I need to beat up for you?"

Madison waved him off. "It's nothing. Just a long day at work."

"Fair enough. Now, if you want to talk about art,

let's talk about those gingerbread cappuccino cupcakes you make." Aaron made an audible groaning sound that a couple of people definitely noticed while walking past.

"Stop," she whispered, "I don't like attention being on me, okay?"

"You just don't have the right kind of attention," Aaron said with a wink. "But back to your cupcakes. Seriously? Can I have them? I would love them."

"Whatever," Madison whispered. "And my cupcakes aren't the best thing I make."

"Now I'm drooling again."

She didn't know what he meant by that, so she moved on. "I could use a cupcake right now. Or cheese. I'm starving," she whispered.

"First off, why didn't you eat a cupcake or something while you were at your café?"

"Because I was working. And when I'm baking, I don't tend to eat."

"I would probably shove my face into frosting if I worked with cupcakes all the time."

"You get used to the fact that you can't because of health reasons. And when it's work, it's not really the same. I could indulge in cupcakes, but I'd rather wait until I'm not standing in my industrial kitchen to do so."

"Fair enough. You have to build your own art first."

"It's not art," Madison said with a shake of her head.

"We can agree to disagree on that."

"Whatever."

"Now, back to cheese."

"We're not going back to cheese."

"I think we do need to go back to cheese."

"Stop saying 'cheese.'"

He grinned. "There is a platter right there. I will make you a perfect plate. Just take a bite."

"Said the serpent to Eve."

"I did offer you an apple on brie, didn't I?" Aaron said with a wink.

"Stop tempting me with dairy. I'll have some when I get home."

"Why won't you have any here?" he asked, his voice soft.

She shook her head, not wanting to go there. "It's not a big deal. Now, go mingle with other people. I'm going to go check on Lincoln."

"You're not going to tell me?"

"There's nothing to tell," she lied, then reached out and squeezed his arm, noticing the muscle. She blushed and moved back.

He noticed her blush and gave her a wicked grin. "Have a good day, Madison McClard."

"It's night," she corrected.

"Well then, have a good night." He practically purred the words before he walked away, and she resisted the urge to roll her eyes again since her mother's friends were watching. Then, she went over to find Lincoln.

Her cousin stood amongst the crowd, looking suave and professional, but she knew that this wasn't his favorite part of the job.

His new agent had built this show for him after Lincoln took a break from doing them for a bit. While she knew it was going well, amazingly well from the comments she'd overheard and the *sold* tags on some of the pieces, she knew that Lincoln would rather be at home painting or cuddling with the two loves of his life.

However, this was part of his job, and he did it well.

The fact that his new agent seemed to understand that and never made him do what he didn't want to, made everything better.

She resisted the urge to curl her fingers into fists at her sides or growl at the thought of his old agent.

Nobody needed to think about him.

"Madison," Holland said, her smile wide as she

came up and kissed Madison's cheek, hugging her tightly.

She sank into Lincoln's girlfriend and closed her eyes, inhaling the woman's sweet scent.

Madison loved Holland.

She was sweet, strong, and took no bullshit from anyone—even if she had a smile on her face when she cut back.

She had dealt with family issues of her own—something Madison was still learning to do—but had come out on top, with not one man, but two.

Considering that one was her cousin, Madison didn't want to say that they were both sexy as fuck. But Ethan was sexy as fuck.

However, he wasn't the sexiest Montgomery in Madison's mind. Then again... She pushed those thoughts from her head since it didn't really matter or need to be in her mind at all.

"Everything looks wonderful," Madison told Holland as Lincoln and Ethan moved forward. Lincoln had his arm around Ethan's waist. When he moved to put his other arm around Holland, Madison noticed a few narrow-eyed glances from people who didn't understand. However, this was an art show, and most artists didn't really care.

The triad in front of her wasn't the only one in their

family, so most of the people attending the event in support understood Lincoln's relationship.

Her parents were not among them. But they didn't matter in the end.

Something she had to repeatedly tell herself.

"Looks to be going pretty well," Lincoln said, looking around.

Ethan snorted. "You're doing fantastic, baby. Stop feeling like you aren't." He kissed Lincoln's cheek, and Madison warmed at the affection. The three of them looked at each other like they were the only people in the world, warmth and perfection surrounding them.

She was only a little bit jealous. Madison wanted a serious relationship, wanted marriage and babies and everything that came with that. She was a baker, a homemaker, and a businesswoman all in one. She wanted a traditional life, even if some of her life wasn't at all conventional.

However, that wouldn't be happening anytime soon, considering that she didn't have time to date, and the men that she *did* go out with were not up to par.

The last one she had dated had droned on and on about his butterfly collection to the point that it had worried her that he might have dead carcasses all over his house. She had been right. They had been everywhere. Staring at her, pinned to the walls, just waiting to gouge out her eyes in her nightmares or something.

While she appreciated hobbies, he had just gotten creepier and creepier over time. After three dates, she called it off.

Much to her parents' disappointment. They had liked the man.

"I'm so proud of you," Madison repeated.

"Thanks for coming, cousin. I know it's not easy for you to take time off since you're the owner of *Sin in a Cup.*"

"We only stay open until eight. And my staff is taking care of things. I just feel like I sometimes need to be there from open to close, no matter what."

"Delegating is the hardest part of owning a business," Holland said, and Madison knew that she understood. Holland owned a small boutique shop in downtown Boulder and did pretty well for herself.

"Anyway, I'm taking up far too much of your time already," Madison said, taking a step back. Lincoln frowned. "Why would you say that?"

Madison shook her head. "You can see me anytime. Go sell some art. Become even more famous." Madison and Holland rolled their eyes, knowing that Lincoln would stay near and not mingle despite his fame.

Lincoln snorted. "Whatever you say."

"I am proud of you. Later, we will celebrate this amazing show."

"With cupcakes?" Ethan asked, his voice sounding as giddy as Aaron's had earlier.

"With cupcakes. I baked you a special batch for your afterparty."

"Yay, something to look forward to," Ethan said.

"I assumed we already had something to look forward to," Lincoln said, his voice low.

Madison blushed to the tips of her ears. "On that note, I'm going to walk away."

Holland laughed, blushing just as hard as Madison.

She made her way through the throngs of people, enjoying the warmth and happiness emanating from the room. So many people loved her cousin's art, and it made her ecstatic. He worked so hard. He might have an immeasurable amount of talent, but he also worked hours and hours for his business and put his blood, sweat, and tears into his art.

And now, people were here to purchase it and talk about it in reverent tones.

She was so damned proud of him.

"Madison," a sharp voice said from behind her. "What do you think you are wearing?"

Madison turned on her heels, steeling herself. Goosebumps pebbled her flesh, and she cursed her natural instincts to run and hide. She was not afraid of the woman in front of her. She couldn't be. And yet, fear coated her.

"Mother."

"What is that atrocity on you? It is hugging your hips and makes you look even wider than you are. Than you could possibly be. The number of cupcakes you eat makes you wide enough. You don't need to accentuate it."

They were in a corner with Madison's father blocking the two of them. Nobody could really over-hear, but she was still embarrassed.

"This isn't the place, Mother."

"Don't you dare talk back to me. And how dare you force Lincoln to invite us when you should have been the one to invite us?"

"What? This isn't even my event. Of course, Lincoln should have invited you. This is his night."

"We are family," Mother snapped. "That is not how things work. You are our daughter. You were the one that was supposed to get us here. Instead, your cousin had to take time out of his precious day with his deviants in order to invite us when we should have already been on the guest list."

"First, you're not making any sense. You're contra-dicting yourself. Second? Don't use that word."

"What? Deviants? We are talking about his proclivities," her mother snipped. "I don't understand why people are so accepting."

"It's not your place to understand. It is not your place to talk about it."

"What did I say about talking back to me? You're lucky we're in public, or I would wipe that smile right off your face."

Madison let out a sigh. She stood up to her mother often, but Mother didn't care. She had only gotten worse the older she got, and as Madison remained unmarried.

"Anyway, since you're here and you won't bother to come over for dinner so we can talk to you, we're just going to have to deal with this now."

"I've been busy. It's a very busy time for my store."

"Yes, your precious little store. Where you just have to indulge in everything you bake."

"Stop it," Madison snapped.

"Whatever." Her mother waved her hand again before she snapped her fingers. "Guy."

Guy? What? Who the hell was she talking about? A guy?

A man wearing a custom-cut suit and a winning smile came over, his bright green eyes flashing. He had perfectly coiffed hair. A single strand delicately flopped over his forehead before he whipped it back, a careless gesture that could have been sexy in any other case.

All Madison felt was meh.

Meh because she had a horrible feeling about this.

"What's going on?" Madison asked, worried.

"This is Guy. Guy, this is the daughter we were telling you about. I wish she had worn the dress I sent over, but there's nothing we can do about that now. This is going to be the woman you'll marry."

Guy smiled, and Madison just blinked, grateful that she wasn't drinking anything or she would have likely choked.

"Excuse me?" Madison asked, confused, angry, and really fucking worried.

"Honey, you're fat. No one is going to love you. Or even want you. And while I understand that that is a curse on our family now, we have found a way to get you to the next stage of your life. As I said, this is Guy. He comes from good, respected family stock, has a great job, and will take you in hand. He is going to be the man you marry."

Madison just blinked, confused, horror sliding over her. Her mother had called her those things before. But marriage?

What. The. Fuck?

"What?" Madison gasped.

"Don't worry. It happens all the time. There are still arranged marriages these days. We found you the perfect match because, apparently, you've been spending too much time on whatever you've been baking,"—baking being code for eating, no doubt. After all, her mother was never subtle—"to find yourself a man."

"No. You can't just tell me who I'm going to marry."

"Do not embarrass me," her mother whispered.

"You're the one who's embarrassing me."

"You will do this. For once in your life, you will do what I tell you and make us proud. Do not be such a disappointment."

Before Madison could say anything, before she could truly understand what was happening, an arm slid around her waist and squeezed her hip. She froze, knowing that touch.

Remembering that touch.

"Madison, baby, there you are." And then Aaron Montgomery kissed the side of her temple and grinned down at her.

Madison blinked up at him, her mouth opening and closing like a fish out of water.

"Excuse me," her mother snapped. "This is a private conversation."

Madison looked up as Aaron raised a single brow.

"Not too private, considering I could overhear you," he growled. Although his voice sounded completely pleasant, Madison heard the warning there.

"Aaron," she whispered.

"No, no, Madison. I think it's time we stop holding our secrets back."

Confused, she just looked up at him.

"Secret?" her mother snapped. Like always, her father simply stood there, quiet.

Madison felt like she should hate them both. But they were her parents. She had tried for so long to be good for them. To understand why they hated her so much.

But it was a lost cause.

"I wanted to talk to you both first," Aaron began. "But I asked, and she said yes. Madison and I are getting married."

Madison blinked, her brain going blank. Her mother gasped, and her father looked nonplussed.

"Married?" her mother whispered, her tone incredulous.

"Married." Aaron looked down at Madison and grinned.

He was such a good actor. Madison saw the warmth in his eyes, even slightly doused by the anger that was also there. "I'm going to marry your daughter, Mrs.

McClard. And that means that guy over there? He's not needed."

"Madison, this can't be true."

Madison heard the anger in her mother's tone. Knew her mom thought that Aaron could never want a girl like Madison. She braced for the words.

"Yes, yes we are."

The lie came out of nowhere, and yet it felt right. And also like a horrible mistake. But she kept her gaze steady.

"That can't be true," her mother continued. "Who would want a girl like you?"

And there it was. Aaron's jaw tightened at those words, and Madison looked over to her mother and raised her chin. "Aaron did. And, yes, he's my fiancé."

And on that note, with that lie, she knew for certain it had been a horrible mistake. However, the look of pure astonishment and hatred in her mother's eyes made it all worth it.

At least she hoped to hell it had been a lie.

CHAPTER TWO

Aaron Montgomery squeezed Madison's hip again and wondered what the hell he was doing. Had he lost his mind?

Undeniably.

He hadn't even realized that he was saying the words until he was suddenly lying to Madison's family as if he did it all the time.

"Oh, really? Convenient," Madison's mother said, her eyes narrowing to cat-like slits.

He did not like this woman. He tried to give most people the benefit of the doubt because he didn't always know the situations behind some people's attitudes or words, but this woman? He hated her.

From what he had heard her say to Madison, she deserved his hatred and more.

"Yes," he said, leaning over to kiss the top of Madison's head. She was wearing heels and yet felt so tiny compared to him.

What would that mean in bed?

He held back a curse. No way would that be happening. Ever. A fake engagement, even if it might not last for more than this conversation, didn't mean they would end up in bed. In fact, because of this fake announcement, they'd most likely never end up in bed —even if he'd had thoughts about it in the past.

No, thank you, he wasn't going to let his thoughts go down that path yet again.

"And you've been hiding this all along?" Madison's mother snapped. "I don't believe this for a second."

"Believe what?" Lincoln asked, coming over to their little corner. Aaron knew the charade would be over now. He'd earned any incriminating looks and yells he received for acting without thinking.

People were starting to stare. Thankfully, some of Aaron's other family members began pulling people's attention away as if they knew that Madison needed a little privacy, even if nothing was private right now. Then his parents began talking to a large group, and Aaron's siblings subtly made their way over.

"Ah, you don't even know?" Madison's mother asked. Aaron thought her name was Maeve, but he couldn't be sure. All he remembered was that she had always been Mother, not Mom, not Mommy, not Ma.

Mother.

"Did you know that Madison and Aaron have been dating? And that they're engaged? No, of course, you didn't. Because it's all a lie. She's a sad, pathetic excuse for a McClard."

Lincoln's eyes narrowed, and Aaron resisted the urge to step forward, but his hand did fist on Madison's waist. She reached around and squeezed his hip as if warning him.

Aaron tried not to think about what that touch meant. Or how much he liked it.

Madison's cousin looked ready to commit murder before he blanked his expression, a sly smile spreading over his features. "Oh, I didn't know we were announcing it," Lincoln said. Aaron froze, his hand spasming on Madison's side. Her hand did the same on him, and Aaron had to wonder what Lincoln would do next.

"You knew?" Madison's mother rasped.

"Of course, I knew. I'm family." Lincoln winked at the barb, and Madison made a little coughing sound that Aaron tried to cover with a laugh.

Aaron leaned forward, smiling. "We were keeping things a little on the down-low because of the new engagements in my family. However, the cat's out of the bag. Considering that you were trying to set up my fiancée with someone else, I had to, you know, make sure my territory was claimed and all that."

"Territory?" Madison asked, her voice so low that Aaron wasn't even sure her mother had heard, despite being so close.

"You...what? A Montgomery?" Madison's mother sputtered.

"Well, look at you, pumpkin." Madison's father spoke for the first time. "Good for you. I guess we don't need Guy." The elder McClard flicked his fingers as if the man should just walk away. Instead, Guy narrowed his eyes, his gaze calculating.

Aaron was pretty sure the man didn't believe them.

He wasn't sure anyone did.

It had been a stupid lie, not even a good ruse. But if it got Madison's parents off her back, he would do it again in a heartbeat.

"Do all of the Montgomerys know?" Madison's mother asked.

"Some do. Not everyone else does," Lincoln lied for them all.

"We were waiting for the right time. Honestly, we just enjoy spending time together. Don't we?" Aaron looked down at Madison, who blinked up at him, a smile on her face. Unfortunately, he couldn't tell if it was real or not.

Considering that it was mostly frozen, he had a feeling there was nothing real about it.

"I guess we'll have to make sure we do everything in our power to make this happen then, won't we?" Madison's mother said, and Aaron had no idea what she meant by that.

"If it's all right with you, I'm going to take the couple away because I want to have Aaron speak to a few people. You know, being in the business and everything," Lincoln said.

"In art?" Madison's mother said slowly.

"Yes, he's very successful. Probably even more so than Lincoln." Madison winked at her cousin, and Lincoln threw his head back and laughed, even as Aaron's smile dimmed a bit.

No, he wasn't more successful than Lincoln. And that was fine, considering they didn't move in the same art circles. But he did well for himself.

The fact that he was now the lamb out for slaughter worried him, though. However, he had put himself in this situation, so he would just have to deal with it.

Anything to help Madison get this woman off her back.

"Well, I'm sure we'll have a lot to talk about," Madison's mother said, her eyes narrowing even further. She looked like a giant snake ready to strike at any moment, and Aaron wasn't a fan.

"Okay," Aaron said, moving his hand from Madison's waist to link his fingers with hers. "We'll see you later." Aaron tugged her away, Lincoln at Madison's other side.

"I'll warn the family," Lincoln whispered.

"What just happened?" Madison asked.

"Let's go outside and talk," Aaron said, really worried that he had just fucked things up beyond recognition.

"The Montgomerys are behind you."

Aaron looked over Madison's head at Lincoln and smiled. "Hell yeah, we are. You're one of us, right?"

"I should say always, but it did take me a while to get here. However, we'll keep up the ruse for as long as you need us to."

"How can you be so sure?" Madison gasped.

"Because it's what they do," Lincoln said.

"He's right," Aaron said as Lincoln nodded and walked over to the rest of the Montgomerys.

Soon, the entire family would know that they were pretending to be engaged.

How long would it last? He didn't know, but he had a feeling he would have to deal with at least some of the ramifications as soon as he stepped outside with Madison. Namely, the slap across the face he imagined would be coming. He deserved it.

And he'd take it. Anything to make her feel better.

It was either come up with this stupid ruse that had come out of nowhere or strangle her mother.

At least this would end up with less bloodshed.

Maybe.

Cool air slid over his face as they stepped out onto the back porch. A couple of people were smoking before they put out their cigarettes and returned to the gallery.

Aaron let out a breath and turned to Madison.

She had her arms folded over her chest and was practically shaking.

"Madison."

She put her hand out in front of her. "I'm going to need a minute. Or like four. Can you do that for me?"

"I can do that," Aaron said, holding back a wince.

Madison started to pace, her blond curls bouncing around her face, her hips swaying in that very provocative way that always went straight to his dick. Not that he'd ever let himself think about that. At least not a lot. And now, just because he was sort of fake engaged for the next thirty seconds didn't mean he was allowed to think about Madison in any way but like a sister. A cousin.

Not a girl he'd had a sex dream about where he fucked her hard against his shower wall, and then went down on her until he woke up, hard and aching—and quite embarrassed.

He studied her face, her high cheekbones, her large eyes that made her look innocent, curious, and sexy as hell. Not that he'd ever tell her that. Her hair was a shade of blond that he loved, though he knew the pink tips at the bottom were hidden amongst the curls so only those who knew they were there could notice them and not think they were just a trick of the light.

He loved that she had color in her hair just for her. But he hated the fact that she had hidden it tonight because of her mom and dad.

"What's up with your parents?" he asked, forgetting that she had told him to keep quiet.

She let out a sigh and shook her head.

"Mark and Maeve McClard come from long lines of good families, good breeding, and sturdy stock."

Aaron's eyebrows rose. "Now you sound like you're literally in the Highlands of Scotland, back in the days of kilts and war."

"They would never be lowlanders, of course. Only Highlanders," Madison said with a roll of her eyes. "I only said those words because my mother *literally* said them to me when she was selling me off to the highest bidder."

"Selling you?" he asked, grinding his teeth.

"She might not have said that exactly, but why would a man like Guy ever come to my side and even agree to the whole arranged marriage thing if not for that?"

Aaron let out a breath and took a step forward, gripping her shoulders.

"What?" she asked, frowning.

"Never, *ever* degrade yourself like that in front of me. A man like Guy? Fuck that. How desperate was he that he was willing to do whatever your mother told him to do?"

"Apparently, *I* do what my mother tells me to do," she mumbled.

"No, you don't. You have the job you want. You own a business. And you're marrying me."

"No, I'm not," she said with a laugh, her voice so low he knew it wouldn't carry.

"Well, my entire family's going with it, so you may have to continue with the charade."

"Why did you do it? Why?"

"I don't know," Aaron said, lowering his hands before sticking them into his pockets.

"That won't be a good enough answer for anyone.

Especially not me. Why did you lie? Because what the hell am I going to do now?"

"I'm sorry I lied. No, fuck that. I'm not sorry. I heard what she said to you. It was horrible. I couldn't just stand there and let her continue."

"I would've stood up for myself."

"Would you?" Aaron asked and immediately regretted the words.

Madison's expression fell, tears filling her eyes. But she shook her head and blinked them away. "I'd like to think I would have. We'll never know for sure. However, that's not the important thing now. The important thing is that my mother and father think we're getting married. What the fuck? What am I going to do? When you dump me, they're going to blame me. How could you do this?"

Aaron rubbed his temples and shook his head. "I wanted to help."

"You didn't. You made it worse. Now they're going to blame me, and they'll lord this over my head forever. I couldn't even stand up for myself. I should have. Only I didn't have the guts to do it."

"Maybe it's time that someone stood up for you," Aaron said, his voice low.

Her eyes widened for a moment. He wasn't sure what he was going to say next. It didn't matter, because the door opened, and Maeve and Mark McClard stepped out.

Without thinking, knowing it was probably a mistake, Aaron stepped forward, put a hand on either side of Madison's face, and lowered his mouth to hers.

She let out a soft breath of exclamation as her eyes widened, but then there was nothing else.

Just her taste on his tongue. It was all he could do to not moan and push her against the railing and beg for more. He plundered her mouth, aching, wanting. She was so small, so deserving of being cherished.

And while he might not be the right person for that, he could pretend for the moment. He could imagine.

"Excuse me," Maeve said with a pointed cough. "We didn't realize we'd be interrupting." Aaron heard the smile in her voice, so he moved away, needing to catch his breath anyway.

"Mother," Madison said, her lips swollen from his kisses, her breath a little choppy.

He'd done that.

Fuck.

That kiss hadn't been fake, at least not on his end.

And...hell.

"You're coming to dinner," Maeve said into the silence.

Aaron frowned. "Excuse me?

"You'll be coming to dinner. We need to meet the man my precious daughter will be marrying."

Aaron heard Madison mutter the word *precious*, and he did his best not to laugh. What the hell was up with this woman? He did not understand this mother-daughter relationship, but he knew that Madison always tried to please her mom, even though he knew the woman didn't deserve it.

He wasn't sure Madison understood that, though.

"Dinner?" Aaron said again. "I can do that. What do you say, baby?"

Madison raised a single brow, something that he was never good at. But it looked sexy as hell on her.

He really needed to stop that line of thinking.

"Yes, dinner," Maeve repeated. "We want to get to know you. After all, you'll be our son-in-law. Imagine that." Maeve narrowed her eyes. "Interesting, isn't it, Madison? That the perfect man just showed up out of nowhere for you, right when we finally found someone that would take you." Her mother paused. "Very interesting."

Before Aaron or Madison could say anything in response, both Mark and Maeve left the porch, leaving Aaron and Madison alone.

"Your mother's a piece of work," Aaron said softly.

"I know. Yet I still love her. And I have no idea why."

"I don't know what to say to that," Aaron said honestly.

"She has good moments. Times when she's not this person. They just seem to be kind of few and far between these days. I don't know. What are we going to do, Aaron?"

"Well, it looks like we're going to dinner."

"That's not what I meant."

"I don't know. I said it to take the pressure off you and to prove that you could have anyone you wanted. Though I sort of put myself out there on a platter, didn't I?"

"It's going to blow up in our faces. And we both know it."

He turned to her then and tucked her hair behind her ears. She looked flushed, confused, hurt, and even a little angry.

He was afraid he was the reason for every one of those.

"How about I come over tomorrow, and we talk it out? We'll figure out what to do."

"I don't want your family to hate me."

He blinked, shocked. "How could they? They love you, Madison."

"But we're going to be lying to them. If we do this. We're going to be lying to them."

"If we do this, it'll be my lie. And they will all under-stand. They'll just blame romantic, silly-headed Aaron Montgomery. Not you."

"There's nothing silly about you, Aaron."

They were both silent for a moment as Aaron tried to think through her words, as he tried to figure out exactly what *he* was thinking.

Instead, he sighed and shook his head. "We'll figure this out. Together. I don't know how long we can keep it up, but maybe we can. I didn't like the way she talked to you."

"I didn't like it either. I don't like it. And I'm going to stand up for myself."

"Good," he said. "And while you're figuring out what to say, I'll be right beside you. And we'll get Guy off your back, too."

"I guess we're engaged, then?" Madison asked, laughing.

"Hey, now you can be a Montgomery. What do you say about that?"

"I say you're moving far too fast. I don't know what I'm going to do, but I need the night to think. Because if we go to Mother right now and tell her it's a lie, she'll never let me hear the end of it. And I can't deal with that. Even if it's your fault."

Hurt sliced through him, and he felt as if he'd

ruined things—something he'd been good at doing recently. "I'm sorry, Madison."

"No, I am. Because you're going to be sorrier when this all blows up in our faces. No one's ever going to believe that you dumped me. My parents sure won't." And with that, she turned on her heel and walked away, leaving him standing there, wondering what the hell he was doing.

Because she had been hurt and bruised and battered for far longer than even he had known her. And he hadn't been able to see the pain until her mother drew it out.

He wanted to fix it. Like so much in his life, he *needed* to fix it.

But he had no idea how to go about it.

And, honestly, he didn't know if he was the right man to do it.

But if he hurt Madison more than she already was? He would never forgive himself.

And he knew his family would never forgive him either.

CHAPTER THREE

"I've always wanted you."

"You've always wanted what?" Madison asked, her breath hitching, her palms damp.

Aaron leaned forward, his breath warm against her lips. "You. I've always wanted you. And now I get to have you. Every curve, every single sexy inch of you. And soon, you'll be riding my cock as I pump into you, my hands digging into your flesh, leaving marks just for you and me."

"You're going to what?" she asked, her voice even breathier.

"I'm going to fuck you. And you're going to like it. You're going to want it. And you'll beg for more. This whole thing? It's what you've always wanted. And now, you have it."

Aaron slid his hand up her thigh, her dress rising over her hips. When he slowly dipped his finger into her wetness, she gasped and then groaned—just as the alarm went off.

She rolled over onto her stomach, tried to blink the sleep out of her eyes, and slowly reached for her phone to turn off the alarm.

"That did not just happen," she mumbled, her voice groggy, her throat dry. "That couldn't have happened," she repeated.

She did not have sex dreams about Aaron Montgomery.

Madison got out of bed and slowly made her way to the shower to get ready for the day and pretend that she hadn't just had a weird-ass dream about somebody she didn't even really know.

Somebody she might be engaged to.

That was neither here nor there.

She wasn't opening up the café this morning; her staff was doing it for her. Brynn was wonderful at what she did, and Madison was grateful that she always had the other woman to help. Having someone she trusted meant that she wasn't the only person who could open and close the shop, and she didn't have to be a micro-manager. Only it was weird to let go of the reins sometimes and not be at the place she had given her heart and soul to.

Even if her parents never understood.

That is enough of that thinking.

Madison quickly got ready for the day and did her best to try and look presentable, even though she hadn't really slept well. She left her hair up, not bothering to do it fully since she couldn't focus. She could try to blame Aaron for the dreams, but she couldn't do that either since that very vivid and detailed dream about him hadn't been the only one she'd had.

No, her dreams had been a little complicated all night. Mostly stress dreams and nightmares where she lost her teeth and things like that. It told her that she needed to focus on the now and not worry about the horror that seemed to be everything else in her life.

Her parents might be awful, but they weren't always.

By the time she was ready to go, she realized that she hadn't even had a sip of coffee and blamed it on the dream.

She made her way into her kitchen and started her cup when the doorbell rang.

She froze, tension running up her body as her palms turned sweaty—like they had been in that dream.

She let her cup brew and went to the front door,

wondering what she should say. What should she do? Aaron was early. They were supposed to talk about this whole marriage thing, even though they weren't going to get married. And here he was, at her house. Early.

Right after she'd had a sex dream about him.

Or at least a near-sex dream.

A foreplay dream?

No, enough of that.

She opened the door and then blinked, relief crushing her, even as she swallowed the disappointment she didn't want to feel.

"Why are you looking at me like that?" Lincoln asked as her cousin made his way into her house, kissing her on the forehead as he passed.

"I didn't know you were going to be here today." Madison closed the door behind him, locking it, wondering why she felt disappointed. She shouldn't. It wasn't like she really wanted Aaron to be here. If she did, then she'd have to think about exactly what they were doing about this whole fake engagement thing.

Dear God, she was fake engaged. Why had she said yes?

"I am here because of what happened last night."

"What? The fact that you sold nearly all of your art? Or that you are an amazing artist who is kicking ass and becoming so famous that I feel like I should bow or something because you're in my house?" she asked glibly.

"Okay, you always were a brat, but you're just getting brattier." He paused, raising a single brow. "Must be what happens when you get engaged to a Montgomery."

She coughed and shook her head. "It's not what you think."

"I thought that Aaron tried to make things better because your mom was a bitch like normal. Sorry for using the word *bitch*, you know I hate it. But come on, she's a bitch."

"You're welcome to use that word when it comes to my mother." Madison shrugged, knowing that she hated the word too, but anyone who had met her mother knew what she was. And there was no changing that.

"As I was saying, I figured Aaron was trying to get your family off your back after they probably said things to you that were rude, crude, and something that I probably would have hit them for. Since I wasn't there, Aaron stepped up to the plate. And, because he is Aaron, and a romantic at heart, he assumed that saying you were taken would get you off the hook."

"Well, aren't you just perfect in every single way? And a great guesser." She knew she grumbled, but she couldn't help it. She didn't like that her family acted so terribly, or that her reactions to her parents were so rote at this point, he knew the routine.

"Who was that man near your mom? What happened?"

"My mother called me some horrible things, like usual, and said it was time I lived up to the family name and did something with my life."

Madison didn't mention anything about what her mother had said about Lincoln. He'd heard it all before, and there was no reason for her to repeat the cruel words and hurt the man Madison adored like a brother.

"And what does that mean?" Lincoln asked.

"She explained it was time for me to get married. Said she had found me the perfect man who could deal with my...let's say, flaws."

Lincoln's gaze darkened. "I'm going to kill her."

"She's your aunt. You can't kill her."

"No, I think that gives me more of a right."

"I don't think the law would agree."

"Fuck the law. That woman. I do not understand how she can be related to the rest of your family."

"My dad isn't much better. But that's just...whatever."

"He wants you to marry that man like your mom does? What is his name anyway?"

"Guy."

"If you can't remember his name, that's fine. But you don't need to call him *guy*. Though he doesn't need a name, considering he went along with this whole thing with your mother."

That made Madison laugh. "No, his name is Guy. He really is *that guy*."

Lincoln's eyes went comically wide before he laughed. "Now it really is a farce. And you're engaged to my brother-in-law."

"Fake engaged. I think. It doesn't matter because Aaron will be here shortly, and we're going to go over exactly what he was thinking and what *I* was thinking, going along with it. It'll all be over soon, and then Mother will go on another tirade and call me a liar or whatever she feels like. Maybe a charlatan. She does like that word."

"Or a harlot. She hasn't called you that in a bit."

"You know, she just might. I don't think she's called me that in a while because I haven't been out with anybody. Hence the whole Guy thing."

"I hate her for you."

"I don't like her most days, either."

"Then what are you going to do?" Lincoln asked, his voice soft.

"I have no idea. But it's going to be fine. We're going

to laugh about it in the end, and everybody will continue thinking that Aaron Montgomery is the best, and that he tried to save the day. But we all know that my parents will never truly believe it, even if they want to nab a Montgomery."

"That was a lot. But first, I nabbed a Montgomery *and* Holland. So your parents can go fuck themselves."

Madison winced, images filling her head that never needed to be there. "Please do not mention my parents and fucking ever again in the same sentence."

"Deal. Also, should we talk about the fact that you seem to have an idea about Aaron Montgomery that I'm not aware of?"

"What?" she asked, truly confused.

Lincoln shook his head.

"Never mind. Clearly, I'm just reading too much into the situation because...hello, you're engaged."

"Fake engaged. And it's going to end soon."

"And then what are you going to do?"

"I'm going to need to figure out how to stand up to my mother and tell her to stop. Aaron was just giving me time to do so because Mother makes everything so difficult. She just steps into my life and takes over, even though I try to stand up to her."

"I know. I know more than anyone what she does. She doesn't give you a choice or a chance. I know she wasn't always this way, so it's hard for you to look back and not see the mom she used to be."

"When did you get so good at reading people?" she asked, shaking her head with a small smile on her face.

"I've always been good at it. Plus, Holland and Ethan always keep me on my toes, so I'm getting better at understanding people. I still don't understand why you let them do what you do, but I get it."

"If you get it, then you *do* understand. And if you don't understand, then you don't get it."

Lincoln snorted. "Fine then. Deconstruct my grammar. I see how it is."

"You just came over here to check on me?" she asked after a moment.

"You're my cousin. Practically my sister. Of course, I'm here to make sure you're okay."

"I can take care of myself."

"Just because you can, doesn't mean you should," he said before kissing her temple again.

The doorbell rang as he pulled away, and Madison froze, having a feeling she knew exactly who it was.

"I didn't realize you were meeting him here. I assumed you'd be going to the café. Or meeting in an open space. Not where you'll be all alone with Aaron."

She raised a single brow, just like Lincoln had. "Excuse me? Why would you have an issue with that?"

"Because you're my baby sister. Sort of. And I can do what I want."

"Don't get all growly with me. It's just Aaron. Nothing's going to happen."

"Sure. Whatever you say." She had a feeling that he didn't believe her in the slightest. And, honestly, she wasn't sure she believed herself.

She went to the door and opened it, then did her best not to swallow her tongue. After all, it wouldn't be good for anybody if she swooned right in front of the man she'd had the sex dream about. No, scratch that. A foreplay dream. Right?

"Hey. Is this the right time?" Aaron asked before his gaze widened. Madison knew that Lincoln was right behind her, hovering. She could feel him, and from Aaron's look, he was either surprised to see Lincoln, or Lincoln was making some kind of rude gesture. She knew the two were friends, but it was still a little worrisome how her cousin was reacting.

"Aaron."

"Lincoln," Aaron said, mimicking her cousin's deep and skeptical tone.

Madison just wanted to crawl into a hole and pretend that none of this was happening. But that wouldn't accomplish anything.

She looked up at Aaron and did her best not to

imagine him as he had been in her dream. After all, that had only been a figment. The idea of everything they had talked about while he was trying to save her behind had simply come back to her in a weird, subconscious way. It didn't mean she actually wanted to sleep with Aaron Montgomery. It just meant that her brain was having a field day trying to figure out how to get out of the situation she was in.

"This is perfect. Come on in. Lincoln was just leaving," she said, putting steel in her voice. She looked over at her cousin, who just rolled his eyes.

"I was. But now I kind of want to stay and see what happens."

"Lincoln. You have work to do. And you don't need to be here for this."

"So you say. But I think I'd have more fun here."

"Out, you brute."

"Ouch," Lincoln said, winking. And then he looked over at Aaron and narrowed his eyes.

"Don't fuck with her."

"Lincoln!" She gasped.

"What? I already said you were practically my sister. You're going to do this to keep the folks off? Fine. But, Aaron? You touch her in any way? You hurt her? You will deal with me."

"I get you. I'm not going to fuck this up."

Madison wanted to crawl into a hole and die. She also wanted to beat somebody up because the embarrassment was almost too much to bear at this point.

"I can take care of myself. I do not need this show of masculine...whatever the hell is going on between you right now."

"I'm just looking out for you," Lincoln said, kissing her on the temple.

"No, you're being a jerk. I'm not going to mess this up," Aaron said again, his gaze on Lincoln's face for a moment before meeting hers.

"I know. I trust you. Plus, it would be kind of horrible if I had to maim you, considering I'm in a relationship with your brother."

"Yes," Aaron said dryly. That would be horrible."

"At least we understand each other. Let us know what happens," Lincoln said as he walked out. Madison closed her eyes, groaning as she ended up alone with Aaron.

"Well. I was not expecting that," Madison said after a moment, looking up at Aaron as he made his way fully into the house.

"Honestly, I was," Aaron said, and she frowned.

"What?"

"Of course, Lincoln would want to make sure that I don't fuck things up. I'd do the same thing for Bristol. I did do the same thing for Bristol. To the point where it kind of got me in trouble with the rest of the family, but somebody had to make sure that Marcus didn't screw things up."

"Bristol and Marcus are best friends. They weren't going to screw things up."

"Well, you and I are friends. Therefore, we're not going to do it either."

Madison paused. "Okay." She took a breath. "That was a weird way to start this. Whatever *this* is."

"Yeah. But now that I'm here, we can figure it out."

"Are we just going to end it? Forget it ever happened?"

"I don't know." Aaron stuffed his hands into his pockets and looked around her small home.

She liked her place, it was hers—and the bank's, but it was mostly hers. Her parents hated it, for the most part because she didn't dress it up with antiques or anything they considered classy. It was a little unconventional, a bit thrift store, but it was all hers. One day, she would have all new pieces rather than things she found secondhand, but for now, this worked for her. After all, she spent most of her time and money on her store rather than herself. And she was just fine with that.

"You know, I've read a few romances that started like this."

Madison groaned, knowing that Aaron loved reading romance novels and thrillers. Basically, anything that was the written word. She admired him for it. She knew that his brothers and some of the other guys came to him for romantic advice, but this was nothing like that. This was something entirely different.

"You know, so have I. But it never really ends well, does it? And we're not in one of those books. And I won't be fucking with you. Okay?"

Aaron's brows rose at her tone. "Fine. We won't fuck. But maybe we can still play around." He winked, and Madison just stared at him, blinking. "What?"

"I'm just saying. We can be smart about each other and how we do this. And we can make sure that we don't kiss. Don't touch. But we can still do what we need to, to keep your family off your back."

"Oh." She was so confused. "What do you mean?"

"We don't have to fuck, or kiss, or do anything like that. I was just kidding about that. Really." He stared at her then, and she swallowed hard. "That's a different way to tease."

"I'm not going to touch on the whole teasing thing.

I think the clearer we are with each other, the easier this will be."

"There's nothing easy about this."

"You're right. There isn't. But if you need time to figure out how you're going to get your mother off your back, I'm here. We can do whatever we need to, to make your family see exactly who you are."

She didn't know what to say to that. She was worried, but she didn't say anything. She was so grateful that she could stand up to her family, and she had to, but this was so out of the blue that she knew her mother would never leave her alone about it. She had already ignored seven phone calls from her mother that morning. There were probably more since she hadn't looked at her phone since she woke up.

Her mother would never let this go. And unless Madison was ready to walk away fully from a family that had been such a huge part of her heart, she needed to figure out how to get her mother on a new path.

"What happens when this falls apart?" she asked, looking at him. He gazed at her. Her eyes fell to his lips as his tongue peeked out to lick them.

She needed to stop looking at his mouth.

"Then you dump me."

"They're still going to blame me, you know. That's sort of what they do."

Aaron's jaw tightened for a moment before he gave her a tight nod. "Then we'll make sure they know you, at least. Not the woman they want you to be. Or...you just walk away. Your choice. But this at least gives you the space to breathe. To figure it out. And it could be fun. Get your mind off the fact that your mother is fucking crazy."

"She is that. I just don't know what will happen."

"Like I said, this gives you time to figure it all out. And it really could be fun. Something to get my mind off my work, too."

"Really? I'm just a distraction?"

"You're anything but, Madison. I can be your friend. And I guess your fake fiancé for now."

She let out a breath and held out her hand, swallowing hard. When Aaron looked at her for a moment, she was afraid that he wouldn't touch her, but then he slid his hand into hers and gave it a squeeze and a shake.

"Okay. This is the weirdest way to begin an engagement. But then again, there might be weirder. So, let's come up with a plan."

They started talking about fake dating and dinners, and precisely what was going to happen.

She did her best not to look at him, not to stare.

And she sure as hell made sure not to think about that damn dream.

CHAPTER FOUR

Aaron scowled at the sketch in front of him, angling his pencil so he could add more shading and get it to the point where he could figure out what he wanted to accomplish with the project.

He had to go into his workshop and start working on this piece soon for a client who only said they wanted something red. Didn't matter what it was, they just wanted something by Aaron Montgomery, and they wanted it to be red. And that meant he had to figure out something that wasn't just a red blob. At this point, that was the only thing he could come up with.

He set down his notebook and ran his hands over his face, annoyed with himself. There was a reason he couldn't focus, why he couldn't get in the mood to get anything done. And that reason was the person he had somehow become engaged to. He wasn't quite sure how it had happened, but he knew it was all his fault. Of course, it was his fault. He was the one who'd started this whole thing, and the one who wanted it to happen.

But why? To be the savior? To be the one who fixed things? That wasn't him. Not really. That was his other brothers, and hell, even his sister to some degree. Aaron wasn't the fixer of his family. He was the one who smoothed things over once the jagged pieces were brought back together by the others. At least, that's what his mom had told him once. The idea had stuck with him.

It didn't matter in the end, though. Because he had a feeling that if this whole fake fiancée thing didn't work out, it would blow up in their faces. And he wasn't sure what he would do.

He pushed those thoughts from his mind, set down his notebook, and went to the other side of his workshop. He had his blowpipe, and his furnace, and everything else set up. The installation had taken a huge chunk of his savings—at least at first. It had been worth it, though. Not having to rent a space or even leave this property to work was priceless. Because, sometimes, he got an idea in the middle of the night.

With the workshop here, he could hype himself up on coffee and get to work.

Even if it was two o'clock in the morning.

Somehow, he'd been able to purchase the land and build the furnace and everything. Not many places would let him do that. But he had been lucky. He'd found a foreclosed building that needed a lot of work and a lot of care, but it had been the perfect price for him.

And, thanks to his career, he had been able to pay it all off. But he had been worried at first that he'd taken too big of a leap.

Now, he was able to work from home, create art, and figure out what pieces he'd like to sell off, which ones he wanted to give as gifts, and others that just ended up on the cutting room shelf.

He never put them on the floor unless they were too large. He had one eight-foot-tall piece that he had named *Wheat,* that he still wasn't done with. He had a feeling if he wasn't careful and didn't find more inspiration for it, it would stay there forever, taunting him with his failure.

He sighed, looked around at what he needed to do, and shook his head. No art would get done today. He might as well work on his books, sketch some more, or call it a day and catch up on Netflix.

Because for now, work just wasn't happening.

He headed back into his house and frowned.

He wanted Madison. That was the problem with all of this. He'd wanted her from the moment he saw her. Had fallen for that smile of hers, those curves, the way she laughed with him—and sometimes *at* him.

He had felt that maybe they could become partners in crime, given their large families. Well, not her family so much as the fact that she was now part of the Montgomerys through Lincoln.

And that counted.

Madison had always been hot as fuck in Aaron's eyes, even if her mother was a bitch who did her best to degrade and put Madison down whenever she could. Aaron had always had the hots for Madison but had never acted on it. After all, she was off-limits. The fact that she and Lincoln were even allowing this charade at all told him that things were far more dire than he even realized. Or, they were just too surprised by everything, so somehow, this was all happening.

He didn't know. But in the end, he would do his best to make sure that he didn't fuck this up. Madison deserved happiness. Even if that wasn't with him in the long run, he could still do his best to ensure that she didn't get hurt right now.

He had no idea how to go about that, though.

Because he had a feeling that even if he didn't hurt her directly, her mother would somehow.

He couldn't fathom how a woman could be so casually cruel, but there it was. And he was going to do his best to make sure that Madison never had to deal with that horror again.

His doorbell rang, and he frowned, thinking who could be at his house after dinner.

He looked down at his phone. No one had called him. He shrugged and made his way to the front door.

He opened it and should have figured who would be there.

Liam, Ethan, and Lincoln made their way inside, pushing past him without even saying a word.

So, this was it. Aaron was either going to get his ass beaten, or they would want details.

And from the glowers on the men's faces, looks mixed with curiosity, he figured it might be a mix of both.

"Guys."

"Hi there," Ethan said, raising a single brow.

"Anything you'd like to tell us?" Liam asked, amusement in his expression. Amusement was good. Amusement meant that he might not get his ass kicked. Right?

"Yes, let's talk," Lincoln said.

Aaron met each of their gazes. "What do you want

to know? We already talked at the show and earlier today." He swallowed hard, a little nervous but also not wanting to get into it too much. After all, this was between him and Madison, and no one else.

Okay, so that was a complete lie, considering who was at his door. But he could tell himself that it was just him and Madison. And, in the end, it was just her. He'd do anything to keep from hurting her.

"Why don't you tell us exactly what you were thinking?" Lincoln said, taking a seat on the couch. The others did the same, taking up positions on different furniture pieces. Aaron stood, feeling like he was on display. He probably deserved it.

"I don't know. I only know I'm an idiot."

"You just said I don't know, and I know," Ethan said. "You're not making any sense."

"I don't know what I was thinking other than that I wanted to make Madison happy." There was silence, and he threw his hands into the air. "Did you hear her mom?"

Lincoln scowled. "I always hear her mom. She's a bitch. And you know I hate using that word."

"We all hate using that word," Liam said.

"I shouldn't have gone in there without a plan, but I saw what her mother was doing, and I felt like I should do something. Even if it was idiotic."

Ethan leaned forward. "It does sound pretty idiotic. To come up and lie about being her fiancé out of the blue?" Aaron looked at Ethan.

"I know. And I can't go back and not lie about it now, because it's already out there."

"You're right. The lie is already out there. So now you're going to have to deal with it," Ethan continued.

"Did her mom believe it?" Liam asked.

Aaron looked at Lincoln. "Did she?"

"I don't know," Lincoln said, rubbing his jaw.

"Well, that's not very helpful," Aaron said and then winched at Lincoln's look.

"I think she wants to believe it because she wants her *precious* daughter to be married to a Montgomery."

"Really?" Liam asked. "Why?"

That made Aaron snort. "You're a former model turned best-selling author. I can give you a few million reasons why."

"Ouch," Liam said.

"Excuse me, I should be the one saying ouch," Ethan said. "Just because I don't make the kind of money you two do, doesn't mean I'm not a desirable catch."

"Of course, you are, baby," Lincoln said, and Aaron snorted.

Before he could say anything else, though, the doorbell rang. Aaron narrowed his eyes, looked around the room, and nodded. "It must be Marcus."

"Probably. He was running late with a project, but that should be him."

At Liam's words, Aaron turned and opened the door to find his future brother-in-law standing there, a glower on his face. "I see they haven't kicked your ass yet, so you must still be explaining what you were thinking doing what you're doing with Lincoln's precious baby cousin." He stormed past, and Aaron let out a sigh.

It seemed today would be the day when Aaron finally got what was coming to him. They had been threatening it for years, and here it was.

"What did I miss?" Marcus asked, taking a seat next to Lincoln.

"Apparently, Madison's mom, Maeve, was being her normal self, and Aaron stepped in to save the day."

Aaron didn't like Ethan's tone and narrowed his eyes. "She was trying to marry her off to a random guy named Guy."

"His name is Guy?" Liam asked.

Ethan held up his hands. "There are nice Guys out there. Guy Fieri constantly raises money for people in need and is always one of the first to help during the forest fires with food and other helpful stuff."

"Okay, okay, Ethan," Liam said. "Guy Fieri is amazing. But Madison's mom wants her to marry a guy named Guy? A guy we don't know. That seems a little too maniacal even for Maeve."

"Tell me about it," Aaron grumbled. "And it wasn't just that, it was that she said horrible things I'm not going to repeat. Things that I wanted to slap the woman for even uttering. And I've never hit a woman."

"I've wanted to hit my aunt a few times, too," Lincoln said, shrugging. "I don't know if that makes me a bad person or someone with restraint for the fact that I haven't done it yet. Madison's parents are horrible. Not just her mom. Her dad is neglectful and lets his wife run all over him and their daughter. He routinely puts Madison in front of him, so he doesn't have to deal with the wrath. I don't know why they're still together, other than the money. I don't know. But that's them. Madison, however, loves her parents. I don't think she likes them all that much, but she loves them. For some reason, she's always felt that she has to be perfect in order to appease them. To make them love her back. I hate that she constantly lowers herself to prove to them that she's worth their affection."

Aaron let his hands fall to his sides. "She opened her café against their wishes. She called it *Sin in a Cup*. That's standing up."

Lincoln met Aaron's gaze, a look of understanding in them—and a bit of curiosity, too. "You're right. She did do all of that. She stands up to them in subtle ways. But she always wants them to love her back. To be the way things used to be."

"What do you mean?" Marcus asked.

"My aunt and uncle used to be better. I don't know what happened, maybe just time or bitterness. But they used to be good. Or at least, not as shitty. My parents used to hang out with them every weekend. That's how Madison and I became so close while growing up. We're like brother and sister instead of cousins."

Aaron heard the warning in that but ignored it, mostly because he had to.

"I think something happened. Or maybe it didn't, and they just turned into who they are now. But Maeve and Mark McClard hate themselves, and they hate their daughter because of it. They tell themselves and Madison and the rest of us that they only want what's best for her, but they put her in situations where she has to hate herself to appease them. And when she fights back, her mother fights harder. I stand up for her, and her mom hurts her even more. And then things get fine, nice even for a while. And so, Madison goes about her day, pretending that everything's okay because, frankly, I think it's easier to do that. And then, Maeve comes back with shit like this."

"I knew it was bad. I heard it. And I know I can't fix it. But maybe I can be a distraction so she can figure out how to walk away. Or her mom can get off her back for a minute so Madison can breathe. She just needs to breathe, you know?"

Lincoln met Aaron's gaze and nodded. "I know. But don't you fucking hurt her."

Aaron swallowed hard and nodded. "I won't. I'm not. It's not like that."

His dick thought otherwise, as it did in most cases when it came to Madison. He had wanted her from day one. But he wasn't going to act on anything. He wasn't going to hurt her like everyone else had. He would be good. Or at least he would try to be.

"I'm not going to hurt her," he vowed.

"Good. Now, I could use a beer. What do you say?" Lincoln asked. The others smiled, nodding.

"I guess you're inviting yourself over for a beer."

"And you know he's got French onion dip. This fool always has French onion dip," Ethan said, jumping to his feet and heading to the kitchen.

Aaron stood, frowning. "That's my French onion dip."

"Score. He also has sour cream and onion!" Ethan called from the kitchen.

"Looks like we're eating here, too," Liam said, making his way over to Aaron. "You doing okay?" he asked.

Aaron frowned. "Of course, I'm doing okay. This is only to get her mom off her back."

"That's a lie. And you hate lying."

"True," Aaron said, rolling his shoulders back, an uncomfortable sensation cascading through him. "But it's for a good cause."

"You're right. Madison is a good cause. And we're all worried that she's going to get hurt, mostly by her family. Not you. You're just an easy person to shout at right now." He paused while Aaron frowned. "But I've seen you look at her." He whispered the words, and Aaron was grateful.

"I was never going to do anything about it." He hadn't let himself even really imagine it. She'd always been off-limits.

"I figured. Because you're honorable. And there was always that sticky situation of Lincoln being in love with Ethan, complicating anything that you might have wanted with her."

"I just want to be a friend. I want to help out." That wasn't a lie, but he wasn't sure it was the whole truth either. Not anymore—not that he could really talk about it.

"We're all going to worry about Madison. And we will all help you with this scheme because we love her. But we love you, too. And I don't want to see you hurt. None of us do. You know Bristol would have been here in a second, too. Hell, so would have Arden and her friends. All of us want to make sure that you're okay."

"I'm fine," Aaron said, his face heating. "You know me. I always bounce back."

"You do. I'm just worried about the one day you don't." And with that cryptic comment, Liam walked into the kitchen where the guys were pulling out beer and chips and whatever other snacks Aaron had in the fridge.

Aaron swallowed hard and listened to their laughter, their deep voices piling on top of one another. He knew he was making the right decision with Madison.

Aaron had to do this. He couldn't back out now. It would only make Madison hurt more.

He just had to deal with the attraction he felt for her. And he had to ignore that kiss.

He needed to forget that he ever wanted something more.

Because if he was going to live this lie, he might as well keep lying to himself, too.

CHAPTER FIVE

S in in a Cup was Madison's baby. Despite her mother's insistence that she go in another direction more suited to the family, it was her *only* baby. She hadn't yet fulfilled her destiny of becoming a mother and wife to someone important. But she always had Sin in a Cup. Her bakery and café, the place where she used up so much of her creative energy and brainpower.

She absolutely loved the job. Adored the fact that she put her blood, sweat, and tears into every ounce and inch of the place.

She had picked the wallpaper—yes, she had wallpaper in some parts. She had selected the paint colors. Had picked the counters and every piece of industrial-strength equipment.

It was all hers.

She loved her little place, even if it wasn't hustling and bustling like some of the companies her friends owned. Hers was a small little niche café where she served fancy coffees and not-so-fancy coffees, but she guaranteed that everything was unique and subtle and crafted for the customer. None of her mugs matched, but she had done that on purpose. She had a few sets of each kind that she wanted, and mixed and matched them depending on size and use. But all of the colors and shapes worked with the aesthetic of the place.

She had to-go cups, but most of the people came and sat for a bit to drink their coffee as if they needed the respite from their days. And she loved it.

Students came from the universities to study, drinking chai after chai or espresso after espresso. She didn't mind because the students that found her place tipped well and always ordered something. She didn't allow people to come in and sit for long periods without ordering, even to use the WiFi. She had put that rule in place immediately, even though she hated being *that* person. But she needed to eat.

The place was set up almost like a loft apartment with split-levels so people could sit in different areas of the café, sipping coffee or eating some of her cupcakes. She had a few other bakery delights, but cupcakes were sort of her thing. She always had at least five different kinds, one of them being her favorite, a lemon buttercream frosting on a chocolate fudge cupcake. That was the one that was on every day, but the other four rotated to fit the theme of the week. People ordered them by the dozens at times, too, so she kept busy. The cupcakes had been a joke at first, something that she just liked to make on the side. Coffee and having a place for people to talk if they wanted to had been her main goal.

But then she had made cupcakes to make herself happy, and suddenly, everybody wanted some.

She didn't mind. She was quite happy with it.

When people started tasting her cupcakes over time, though, the demand had increased, and she had sort of become known as having coffee in a cup, and then cupcakes in a cup. Hence the name of her café: Sin in a Cup. It was perfect for her.

She had come into it by luck, even though she had good enough business sense to keep it going. Plus, she loved her job. Even if her parents didn't understand why she was happy being part of the working class.

She shuddered at the thought, not wanting to think about them. Her focus needed to be on her cupcakes and finishing up the frosting for the next batch going into the display case.

Today was all about the strawberry cheesecake cupcake with a lemon cream cheese frosting. It was light and airy despite being cheesecake. And so yummy.

Thankfully, she didn't taste her wares every day or she'd have to roll out in a sugar coma. But she was fine with that.

Her family came from old money. On both sides. Hence why her parents had even gotten married. She hadn't realized that arranged marriages were so prevalent these days. Still, apparently, they came out of nowhere and slapped you in the face. Her parents had been one of those, and now her mother wanted Madison to follow tradition and marry a man named Guy.

Well, that just wasn't happening. For many reasons. The main one being that, for now, Aaron had put himself in the crossfire as her fake fiancé.

She shook her head, wondering how she had gotten herself into this situation.

Maybe if she were able to stand up for herself, this wouldn't have happened.

Only she had tried. Every time, her mother just railroaded her. At one point, Madison had even tried cutting her family out of her life completely, but then her dad had gotten sick, and she ran right back to them, needing to be close.

She hated that she still loved her family.

What an odd thing to think: that she hated that she loved.

But that was the situation they had put her in, and there was no coming back from that.

Not really.

Her dad was healthy now, and nobody talked about it. They made it seem as if it had never happened—something she knew her mother wanted to keep going. Madison wasn't sure she could forget how frail her father had looked when he was ill. And that was why she kept coming back. Because she didn't want to see him sick. Her mother, either, honestly. Couldn't even bear to think of it.

But her family didn't love her like that, not the way she needed. Only Lincoln did, and he couldn't stand her parents. Had even cut them out of his life as much as he could.

The only reason he still dealt with them at all was because of her. And it was something she wasn't proud of.

She just wished she was strong enough to walk away. But, occasionally, she got some good glimpses. They weren't always all bad.

She just had to remember that.

Or maybe she needed to forget.

"Hey, Madison, your mom's here."

A feeling of cold water doused her veins, and she swallowed hard.

Oh?" she asked, turning with the frosting bag in hand.

"Yes, and giving us her standard glare since we won't let her come back."

"She should know that she can't come back here. This is a place of business. Plus, it's not safe for her."

"We tried to tell her that. But, honestly, we're a little scared of her. You want to go out front and deal with her?" Brynn asked. Madison nodded, handing over her piping bag after she'd washed her hands.

"Thanks, I'll do it."

"You're a better woman than me," Brynn said, and Madison shook her head.

"We both know that's not the case."

"Hey," Brynn said. "Don't be mean to yourself."

"Sorry, just getting prepared."

Brynn's eyes darkened with sympathy, and Madison hated it. So, she smiled and made her way out to the front of the building where people were drinking coffee and ordering cupcakes and even a few of the cookies that Madison sometimes made. Brynn liked making them, so they had more of them than usual. It was good that they weren't a full bakery. There wasn't a lot of room in their tiny little shop. Something that her mother mentioned. Often.

Madison checked her reflection in the mirror for any stray traces of frosting or cake. She was grateful that she looked decent, though likely not to perfection like her mother wanted. She didn't care.

She straightened her apron, something her mother never wanted her to wear. Yet again, she didn't care. She walked around the corner and saw her mother standing near the bay window, her chin raised, her pearls glistening under the lights.

Her mother was gorgeous. Always had been. When Madison was a little girl, her mother had smiled more. She had thought her mother a fairy princess. One who helped her defeat the dragon until they could ride away on horseback and smile and laugh.

She had never been so wrong about anything in her life.

Her mother must have sensed her approach and turned on her very tall heels, a single brow raised.

Maeve McClard rarely smiled anymore. She only deigned to do so when she needed something from someone lately. And even then, it wasn't a true smile that reached her eyes, it was more of a sneer. Not that anyone who hadn't known her for all of their lives would even notice. Madison did.

Mostly because the sneers were usually cast in her direction.

"Madison."

Madison smiled, aware that no one was paying attention to them, but this was her place of business. "Mother, come to the side over here where there are fewer people."

"I cannot believe you're making me come into this establishment." The way her mother said the word *establishment* made it sound like she was in a roach-infested hotel with slime on the walls and people being murdered all around her.

Sin in a Cup was cute, very clean, and people enjoyed themselves.

Madison would not let her mother ruin this for her. At least she would do her damndest.

"Come with me if you want to talk. If not, then have a wonderful day. I'm working, I don't have too much time..."

"Working. Here." Maeve whispered the words as if aware she didn't want people to overhear her acting like she currently was. Her mother did have a reasonable sense of self every once in a while. Mostly, she didn't like to make a scene if she wouldn't come out on top.

Her mother lifted her chin and followed Madison

towards the back area, which was a little more private and empty. A larger party had left about ten minutes ago, and others were already comfortably seated so they hadn't ventured to the back yet. The sound of her mother's high heels against the wood floor echoed in Madison's head, and she hated what she heard. Disappointment in each step.

Or maybe she was overthinking. That had always been her problem. Or one of them, at least according to her mother.

And that was a known fact.

"So, where's your ring? Doesn't an engaged woman need a ring?"

Apparently, they were going to start right away—no dancing around the subject.

"I'm baking. You know I don't wear jewelry when I bake."

Not a lie, but Aaron hadn't gotten her a ring. And they hadn't talked about it. *Crap*. Engaged people needed rings to show others that they were engaged.

It was something she would have to mention to Aaron. Something that she'd probably have to worry about herself because she wasn't going to force him to buy her something. She could find something fake that looked real. She had jewelry, countless rings and earrings and things that her family had given her over the years. Stuff she treasured but didn't wear that much because it didn't make sense at her place of employment.

Her mother might recognize it if she chose one of those pieces, or she wouldn't care either way because she didn't believe any of this. Even if she wanted Madison to quote, unquote bag a Montgomery.

"That's a nice excuse. You're baking." She sneered the word *baking*, but again, Madison was used to that. Her mother had never understood the things that Madison loved.

Madison wasn't even sure her mother really loved her.

"Is there something specific you wanted?"

"You're not going to talk about it?"

"I don't know if there's much to talk about, Mother."

Her mother snarled, just a slight one before she put her face back to its resting position. "Well, you'll be happy to know that Guy should be here at any moment."

"Guy?" Madison asked, confused.

"Guy. The man you're going to marry. Not Aaron Montgomery."

"What? No. You're not going to set me up, Mother. I appreciate that you want to find me someone that will make me happy," she lied. "But I've already found someone."

That was also a lie. But what was she supposed to say?

"Guy is handsome, comes from a good family, and has money. You won't want for anything. It's about time you step up, take care of your responsibilities, and stop acting like a spoiled child."

"I have a job. A business that I own. I don't take anything from you. How on earth is that me acting spoiled?"

"I put a roof over your head, young lady. You need to listen to me."

"I'm grateful that you did the bare minimum to raise me, but I'm sorry. I'm not going to marry someone I don't know."

"So you're going to keep up the charade about Aaron Montgomery? He might be a catch, but you'll never be good enough for him."

Madison ignored the verbal slap and the pain that slid through her. "And yet you think I'm good enough for Guy?"

"Oh, you're not. But he understands his place, just like you will."

"I just...you need to go." Madison ignored the hurt filling her, the rage that mixed with it. She was just so tired.

But her mother never let up. And her dad didn't care. Why did she keep putting herself in this situation? Oh, yes, because somehow, she still loved them despite everything.

Why couldn't she just make it stop or let go?

"Please go. My shop is not the place for this. There is *no* place for this, honestly. Just go."

"Why don't you understand that I'm just trying to help?"

Madison didn't know why her mom kept doing this. It didn't make any sense, yet nothing her mother said these days did.

"Hey, Brynn said you were back here," Aaron said from the doorway. Madison froze for the barest instant before relief flooded her. She hated herself a little bit that she felt the weight lift. She had been standing up to her mother, had been trying to do her best. But in the end, her mom wouldn't listen. Yet with one sentence from Aaron Montgomery, relief filled her. Her mother turned, her focus on him now rather than Madison.

Why couldn't she just fix what was going on with her family?

Or maybe there was nothing to fix. Nothing left to put back together.

That wasn't a happy thought at all.

Aaron came to her side, nodded at her mother, and

then kissed Madison square on the lips, running his hand down her back. She tried not to lean into him, crave a better taste, or do anything but hold back the moan that threatened to escape.

Why was that little action, something that seemed as if they had done it a thousand times before, making her feel as if she could swoon? She was not someone who swooned.

"Hi," Aaron said, his voice low and husky.

"Hi," she said and then cleared her throat as she moved away. Aaron slid his hand over hers and squeezed her fingers. "As I said, Brynn said you were back here, so I made my way over. Hello there, Mrs. McClard. How are you doing?"

"Aaron."

"You guys having fun back here? Have you tried the double chocolate sin cupcakes that Madison has up there? I might have to take half a dozen home, just for myself. I'm in the middle of a project, but I could use a sugar rush."

"Those are decadent," Madison said, smiling. Warmth filled her at Aaron's compliment, and for some reason, she knew that he was serious. Aaron did not lie; that was who he was. The fact that he was lying about this whole charade of theirs worried her. He didn't exaggerate anything when it came to the details in his life.

She figured he must really love her cupcakes.

She really shouldn't feel so much joy about that.

"I don't eat cupcakes," her mother said, her tone icy. "I see you're going to keep up this little deception."

"Deception?" Aaron asked. "Oh, I get it. You don't believe the news of our engagement. Understandable. We were keeping it a secret for so long that it does seem a little out of the blue. I'm sorry for that. However, that does remind me of something." Aaron turned and pulled something out of his pocket. Madison's eyes widened as she looked down at the velvet box in his hand.

"What?" she breathed.

"I know you don't wear jewelry when you bake, but I figured you could at least wear it around your neck. Maybe next time you won't leave it on my nightstand." He winked at that, and she felt her face heat from the blush.

Aaron Montgomery had just insinuated, in front of her mother, that she had slept over at his house.

Where was a hole so she could crawl in and bury herself?

"Aaron," she whispered.

"No, no. If I'm going to give you a chain with this

ring, I should do it right." And then he went down on one knee in front of her. She blinked down at him, wondering what the hell was happening.

A gasp sounded from the doorway, and Madison looked over to see Brynn and some of her other staff members and a few regulars standing there. Their gazes were filled with wonder and tears. A few people had their phones out.

Dear God. So this was going to be a thing. Something she couldn't take back.

But she had seen the nearly hopeful and perhaps a bit confused look on her mother's face, so Madison wouldn't walk away from this. Because maybe her mom would back off just a bit and they could find a happy medium with their relationship.

That was why she and Aaron were doing this, after all. She turned back to Aaron, her hands clasped in front of her as if afraid to touch anything. When he lifted the lid, she sucked in a breath.

It was gorgeous. A beautiful diamond with small pink stones surrounding it in an antique setting. It looked as if it had been made just for her, and it seemed...real.

"Aaron," she whispered.

"I work with glass every day, and I create art, but I couldn't get this ring just right for you, not with the stones involved. However, when I saw it, I thought of you. Maybe one day you'll let me design something else special. But for now, will you marry me, Madison McClard?"

Someone gasped, and she knew it had to be Brynn.

How would she explain to them that this was fake?

Or should she?

How had she let this get so complicated?

"What do you say?" Aaron asked. "I mean, I've already asked you before, but..." he whispered.

The lie.

The deception.

None of this was real.

What she felt blossoming in her heart for this man on one knee wasn't real either.

Was it?

"Yes, of course. Of course, I'll marry you."

He grinned and then stood up, pulling the ring out of the box. That's when she realized that it was indeed on a chain. He smiled and slid it over her head so the ring landed against her chest, nestled between her breasts.

Aaron gave her a grin that told her he knew exactly where the ring had landed, and she could've pinched him just then. Instead, she just looked up at him and wondered what the hell was happening.

She was shell-shocked, couldn't even focus, but people were cheering and laughing and crying. Her mother was silent, staring at the two of them as if she were seeing them for the first time.

Madison felt like she *was* seeing Aaron for the first time.

No, no, no, no.

This couldn't be happening. She could not be falling for her fiancé. That was against the rules. It had to be.

"Well, then. You'll come to dinner. Tomorrow. No excuses." And on that pronouncement, her mother made her way out of the room, people giving her a wide berth. Madison stood there, turning her head to stare at Aaron, who just grinned.

Aaron.

Her fiancé.

Her lie.

And the man she couldn't let herself fall for.

CHAPTER SIX

aron hoped he wasn't supposed to wear a tie for this. He wasn't sure there was a dress code for an uppity, most likely horrendous family dinner for your fake fiancée.

There was no manual for this, even if Aaron had read a few books where the idea had been introduced. In those, no one cared what you wore because you were too busy being stressed out about what to say and where to sit. You were too worried about the feelings you had for the person at your side, rather than whether you should have tied a piece of fabric around your neck.

Somehow, Aaron was able to worry about it all.

Even if it made him feel a bit like he was losing his mind.

He looked at himself in the mirror, smoothed his shirt, and slid his jacket over his shoulders.

Why was he doing this again?

Oh, yes. To make sure that Madison knew that she was cared for, and to give her time to breathe after an insanely horrible interaction with her mother.

So why then did he feel like he was making a horrible mistake?

It had to be the idea of the tie. *That* was why Aaron had all of these oddly confusing thoughts.

No other reason.

He ran his hand over his newly clean-shaven face and grimaced. He usually liked having a full beard, or at least a bit of scruff, but he'd shaved for her. He wasn't even sure what Madison preferred. Not that it mattered. Because they wouldn't be doing anything with each other.

They were only friends. This whole thing was just them being friendly.

And if he kept telling himself that, he might actually believe it.

No, it was the truth. It couldn't be anything else. It wasn't safe for it to be anything else.

He was doing this for Madison.

He made his way to his car after picking up flowers for Maeve and then steeled himself for the evening.

This was not going to be fun. It would probably be horrible. But at least he'd have something to talk about later with his family.

That wasn't a good enough reason to do this tonight, but Madison needed him. So, he would make it work.

Ten minutes later, he pulled up in front of Madison's house, grateful that she lived close to him. Her parents lived on the other side of the city in a gated community and had a larger house than even Liam.

He shook his head. He was letting his thoughts trail because he didn't want to do what he needed to do tonight. He just wanted to go home and read a book or turn on a movie and let his mind go in a direction where he could focus on his work later. But that wasn't what Madison needed. Though he wasn't sure either of them knew what she needed. Not really. Regardless, he would be by her side to try and help.

And he'd try not to think about her naked. Yes, that was an essential part of his plan tonight.

To not think about Madison naked.

His cock filled at the thought, and he looked down at it, cursing.

"Nope. We are not doing that today. Got it?"

Now he was scolding his dick. There was something seriously wrong with him.

Aaron pushed those weird thoughts from his mind, got out of his car, and made his way to Madison's front door. He knocked quietly, almost as if afraid she'd answer. When she opened the door, she smiled at him, and he saw that her eyes were wide with the same kind of panic he felt.

He should probably stop swallowing his tongue and say something.

She looked gorgeous.

Absolutely stunning.

Even if it was a conservative dress that went past her knees and capped her shoulders without even a hint of cleavage. It still showcased her curves to the point that he had trouble thinking.

"Hi," Madison said, and Aaron swallowed hard.

"Hey. You look great."

She rolled her eyes. "I look like a secretary from the fifties, but that's fine. It's the best dress I have that my mother would approve of."

He raised a brow.

"I don't usually care what I wear, but considering that we're going over as a couple to this thing, I didn't want to add more fuel to the fire by wearing something I actually like."

"And here I was, thinking that you looked fucking fantastic. I apologize for being wrong."

Her cheeks flamed, and he wanted to reach out and brush his knuckles across her skin to see if he could cool her down.

Instead, he made sure his hands were at his sides and nodded.

"You ready to go?" he asked.

"Yes, I am. You look great too, by the way."

Aaron just shook his head. "I spent forever trying to decide if I needed a tie. This is like the weirdest prom ever."

She gave him a look and then threw her head back and laughed.

"Where's my corsage, then?"

Aaron snapped his fingers and shook his head. "I knew I forgot something. I almost brought you flowers, but then I thought that was weird. I do have flowers in the car, but they're for your mom. And now I feel even weirder."

"Oh, that's so sweet. And you were right to not get me flowers. Mostly because I'd have no idea what to do with them because I don't think I have a vase right now."

"We're bad at this, aren't we?"

"Considering I don't know what *this* is and there's no path? Maybe we're doing okay."

Aaron smiled and held out a hand. When she took

it, he did his best not to cheer. They were just friends, one doing a favor for the other. That was all they needed to be.

"Okay. Let's do this."

"We can run away and never deal with my family again if you'd like?" she said quickly. Aaron froze, giving her hand a squeeze as he shook himself out of his reverie.

"Is that what you want to do? We can go elope right now if you want." He was only joking, but given the way her eyes widened, he was afraid that she didn't get the joke. Hell, he wasn't sure *he* got it.

"What do you want to do, Madison? I'm in. No matter what."

"I just want to get this over with so my mother can lord the fact that she thinks we're lying over me. Which we are. But maybe they'll give me space so I can breathe and not have to deal with them. Because, Aaron? If I walk away right now... If I never talk to them again? It won't matter. They'll still find me and judge me. This way, hopefully, it will get them off my back."

"That's why we're doing this. I'm here for you. That's what friends are for." He helped her into the car and tried not to think about why his chest constricted at that statement. They *were* friends. That's why they were doing this. They didn't need to be anything more than that. Sure, they were engaged, but it wasn't real.

They were silent during the car ride. It was completely awkward, and he didn't know what to say.

"They're going to ask questions."

"They are," he said. "And we can tell them the truth as we have been. Our version of it anyway. That we're friends and met because of Lincoln—a person they know."

"And don't necessarily like," Madison added.

"Their loss. They're just assholes." Aaron ground out the words and sighed. "That's probably not the best way to start this thing. They know how we met. They know that we hang out. Because we do. Just because your mom doesn't believe this as of yet—which sort of makes sense considering it was out of the blue—that doesn't mean we can't try to pull it off. It's why we're here. We're going to make it believable. Which means you need to stop freezing every time I touch you."

She gave him a look as they pulled up to the gate. "I do not flinch."

"You do. Then again, I freeze every time you reach out and touch me, too. It's something we're going to have to get over."

He reached through the window and punched in the code that Lincoln had given him. The gate started to pull back, and he looked over at Madison, noticing that her eyes were wide. "Maybe we should've talked about this before. They're going to know. More than they already know."

"I know." He smiled at that. "And that was a whole lot of knowing just now."

"Should I say I know, or should I just keep going over the fact that we're going to get caught? They're going to hate me even more than they already do."

Aaron slowed to a crawl on their way to the house. "If they hate you so much, and you truly believe that, then why are we doing this?"

That was honest. Yes, the idea of a fake fiancée and all the stuff that came with it sounded fun and was an interesting way to get out of the typical day-to-day gloom, but it was a lie. And Aaron hated lying.

"I don't want to lose them forever. And I know that makes me sound a little bit sad—the fact that I can't just walk away. But they used to be so sweet and amazing. I figured maybe if they saw that I was happy, finally, they'd go back to the way things were."

Aaron was silent for enough time that Madison started to squirm in her seat.

"I hope that's true. I hope this gives you some form of peace. And you know what? I'm going to make sure that happens. Because, fuck this."

That startled a laugh out of her.

"Fuck this?" she asked, still laughing.

"Yes. Fuck this. We're going to make this work. We're going to be the best fake engaged couple ever. And I'm going to hold your hand and hold the door for you. And then I'm going to pull your chair out for you. I'm going to be amazing. The world will be jealous that I am not their fake fiancé."

"I'm pretty sure some are already jealous," Madison said dryly.

Aaron pulled into the circular driveway and gave her a startled look. "What?"

She waved him off. "Brynn and the girls at the café already chitter and get all swoony over you. The fact that I'm the one who 'tagged' you?" She used air quotes on the word *tagged*, and Aaron barked out a laugh.

The two of them laughing was the first thing Madison's family heard from the front steps. The McClard valet—yes, they had a valet for the evening—had opened the doors to Aaron's car, and their laughter was clear for all to hear.

Well, then. That was a good way to start. Wasn't it?

Aaron quickly got out of the car, gave the keys to the valet, and went to Madison's side. She was already halfway out and just smiled, sliding her hand into his offered palm as he helped her out.

He had his jacket and the flowers in his other hand and knew he likely wasn't making the best impression, but they were laughing. And when she leaned into him, her eyes bright, he couldn't help but think that maybe this was working.

The ruse.

Nothing else.

Nothing else needed to work.

You ready?" Aaron whispered.

"Always."

They held hands as they ascended the stairs. Madison's parents stood in the overly large doorway, the glass archway stunning though very intimidating—probably precisely what they intended.

"Mother, Father," Madison said, her voice deceptively light.

"Madison. Aaron."

Aaron resisted the urge to clear his throat before making sure Madison was steady on her heels before handing the flowers over to Madison's mother. They were not grocery store flowers, they were hothouse lilies, ones from a very fancy nursery nearby. One of his friends knew the owner and had been able to get in and find out exactly what Maeve McClard preferred. Aaron saw the surprise on her face for a bare instant before her eyes cooled, and she took the flowers with a nod.

"Thank you, Aaron."

"Thank you for welcoming me into your home," he said, his voice pleasant. He squeezed Madison's hand before her parents moved back, welcoming them into the house.

"You have a lovely home," Aaron said.

"I know. We worked long and hard on it. It's our pride and joy. Much like Madison here. Well, much like she was anyway."

At that pointed remark, Mrs. McClard handed over the flowers to her maid, who stood nearby, before gesturing towards the sitting room.

"Come. We can meet our other guest."

Aaron frowned, but Madison spoke up first. "Guest? I thought you just wanted us here for dinner."

"Of course, we do. But why would we want just the two of you?" Maeve's heels tapped on the marble as she made her way, her husband right behind her.

"I have a bad feeling about this," Madison whispered.

"We can still escape. I may have to tackle the valet for the keys, but we can make it work."

"Let's go," she whispered. Aaron took a step back, trying to tug her away, but she stood firm.

"I lied. We have to go in. We can't run."

"No, we can't, but I'm always that option for you."

She gave him a look that went straight to his dick, and he did his best not to let it get to him.

Getting a hard-on in this situation would only lead to horrible things.

Painful stuff.

"Madison," her mother snapped from the other room.

"Let's join the inquisition," Madison whispered.

"Because nobody expects the Spanish Inquisition?"

They were laughing again as they made their way to the parlor. When they entered the room, Aaron nearly choked on his spit.

Guy stood near the window, a glass of whiskey in his hand, joking joyfully with Madison's father.

Aaron hated the guy. And yes, his name, as well.

"Mother?" Madison asked, confusion in her tone.

"You both know Guy. He is such a wonderful family friend. We figured he'd be a perfect dinner guest to join us tonight. After all, Madison does need to explore her options."

"*Options*?" Madison mouthed, and Aaron squeezed her hand again.

Tonight was going horribly.

Seriously bad.

Aaron had not been wrong. Horrible wasn't even the beginning of it.

It started with Guy and continued with the fact that he had been sat at the opposite end of the table from Madison, near her father. Guy got to sit next to Madison, and Aaron hadn't been able to do anything to stop it. If he had tried, he'd have likely made a scene, and everything would have been ten times worse.

When the appetizers showed up, everybody got a delicious and perfectly flakey pastry filled with cheese and meat. Madison got a lettuce wrap.

She shook her head when Aaron opened his mouth to say something. Instead he sat back and watched as her mother treated her like she was nothing. Not intelligent enough to think for herself. And not able to make her own choices.

Madison tried to bring the conversation back around to happy things, tried to remember the good times, and was even nice to Guy. All the while, Aaron held his tongue, wondering what the fuck was going on.

When dinner was served, Madison wasn't served potatoes. And when dessert was offered, she declined. He had a feeling that she wouldn't have been able to have it anyway.

Madison was gorgeous. Yes, she had curves, and he fucking loved them.

She wasn't slender like her mother, but the two had

different bone structures and body shapes that worked for them.

The fact that Madison's mother was not so subtly fat-shaming her? Jesus Christ, Aaron was ready to murder someone.

But Madison took it, the hurt in her eyes so perfectly hidden that he wasn't sure anybody but he had seen it.

When it was time to leave, Aaron could barely speak through his rage, and his hands were shaking.

They got into the car without even a true goodbye or an offer to visit again. He had no idea if the pretense had worked, and honestly, he didn't fucking care. He was too angry.

They made it out of the neighborhood without Aaron speaking a single word. Madison sat still and looked at her hands.

He pulled off the road to stop at a local neighborhood park, let out a breath, turned off the car, and got out.

"Aaron?"

"I need to breathe."

Madison got out and started to pace next to him, her hands in front of her as she stood still after a moment.

"I'm sorry about tonight. It didn't work out the way it should have, did it?"

"Why? Why did that even happen? How could you just sit there and let your mother do that to you? And why did I do nothing and let it happen?"

Aaron had never been this angry before, nor had he ever felt so helpless.

He had tried to speak up during dinner, to defend her. Every time he moved to speak, Madison shook her head and pleaded with her eyes.

And he had done nothing.

He was just as complicit in her pain, and he hated himself for it.

"I'm sorry, Aaron. I'm so sorry."

"Are you fucking kidding me? No, you don't get to be sorry for this. It wasn't you."

"I know, but I'm used to it. If I let Mother do what she wants, it goes quicker, and we usually end up having a pleasant evening. It just didn't turn out that way tonight because she was still trying to set me up with Guy—with my fiancé in the room."

Madison looked down at her finger, the moonlight shining off the diamond. He just snorted.

"So, you let your mother treat you like shit. You let your father passively-aggressively do nothing to stop it. And you call that a pleasant evening?"

"They're not always that bad."

"Could've fooled me."

"They're not. She was being particularly icy tonight, probably because she's not getting what she wants. But she's not that bad. Not all the time."

"I don't know if I can believe it. Why does she continue to demean you? Why do you want her approval?"

"Because they're my family." Desperation filled Madison's eyes. "Other than Lincoln, I have no one. I don't have friends from middle school or high school or even college that I see anymore. People change, and it's tough for me to make friends to begin with. I'm weird and awkward, and I'm sometimes so focused on work that I lose touch with people. But I've always had my family. Yes, they've gotten worse over time, but they're still mine."

"You're better than this, Madison. You're sexy as fuck. You're smart. You're sweet. And you would do anything for your friends. I just don't understand why you don't see that."

Aaron's chest heaved as he tried to get through his anger. But before he could say anything else, Madison rose to her tiptoes, her hand on his cleanly shaven face, and her lips on his.

Aaron didn't stop to think. Instead, he wrapped his

arms around her, gripping her tightly against him, and deepened the kiss, her mouth parting for his. He ravaged her, needing her taste, her touch. Just needing her.

This was a mistake, but he didn't fucking care.

He had her in his arms, her taste was imprinted on him, and yet he craved more.

When he pulled back, both of them breathing heavily, he swallowed hard.

Her lips were swollen from his kisses, the bruising force of the impact making his knees go weak. She looked up at him, blinking.

"Oh."

"Oh," Aaron echoed. "I actually didn't mean to do that."

"I think that's my line." She paused for a moment while Aaron tried to collect his thoughts. "You were standing up for me like that, and...I didn't know what to do. Sorry."

"Please don't fucking say you're sorry again tonight."

"Fine, I'm not sorry. Though I don't think kissing you was the most appropriate action."

"I think of all the things that happened tonight, that was probably the most appropriate."

"Aaron?"

"I think we should keep doing this. If we're going to keep up this charade, I think I want to keep kissing you."

It was a mistake, a horrible one. Something that would hurt them both in the end. Part of him hoped that she'd say no. That she'd push him away and laugh it off.

But when she rose to her toes again and brushed her lips against his once more, he was lost.

So fucking lost.

And, honestly, he wasn't sure if he wanted to find his way out again. Ever.

CHAPTER SEVEN

Aaron leaned against the deck railing and looked at the forest beyond. They were at Liam's cabin in the woods, although hopefully without the horror stories. He inhaled the sweet scent of nature and food, the smoker and grill working overtime behind him.

He was exhausted after not being able to sleep well the night before. Worry and stress over what the fuck he was going to do with Madison had kept him awake. As well as the fact that he'd had sex dream after sex dream about her.

He was going to hell, a fiery one that wouldn't smell as good as this. And it was all his fault.

Given that Madison's cousin, the person most likely

to send him *to* that hell, stood a mere two feet away, his nerves were stretched tight.

"You want to talk about it?" Lincoln asked, lifting the beer to his lips to sip quietly.

Aaron shook his head. "Talk about what?"

Aaron wanted to talk about many things, and he was usually the talker of the group. Ethan might speak at a faster pace, but Aaron was often the one with random topics.

It was just...he wasn't sure what to say today.

"How about the fact that I hear you're an engaged man?" Benjamin said from behind him. Aaron turned to see his cousin walking towards him.

Benjamin was one of his family from Fort Collins. Sadly, he didn't see him often.

Even though they didn't live that far away, between work, family, and life, the two sets of cousins rarely saw one another beyond video conferences and stolen weekends.

Aaron liked Benjamin and was happy that his cousin had been able to make his way to the mountains.

"That's me, engaged," Aaron said, taking a sip of his beer.

"We heard it was fake," Ronin said. Ronin was a friend of Marcus's and new to the group.

This evening was a guys' night, one where they'd have meat, maybe a vegetable or two, and drink a whole shit ton of beer. There were enough rooms in Liam's cabin—considering that it was basically a log mansion in the woods—so nobody even had to bunk together.

None of them had to worry about driving home, so they were going to drink too much, overeat, and likely snore.

Ethan and Lincoln would be sharing a room, of course, and Aaron was grateful that his room was on the other side of the cabin. He was pretty sure those two wouldn't stay quiet all night.

And some things a brother just did not need to hear. Ever.

"Are we telling everybody that it's fake?" Aaron asked, giving Marcus a disappointed glare.

"I only told Ronin about ten minutes ago, and it was because he asked and sounded excited. I'm not going to lie to my friends. Sorry."

Aaron frowned. "Fine. But nobody else."

"I shouldn't tell my siblings?" Benjamin asked, grinning. "Because they're getting excited about the wedding. All of the weddings, in fact. You Boulder bunch keep getting hitched. But if this one's fake? It may put a damper on the whole thing."

Aaron finished his beer and was grateful when Ethan handed over another without him having to say anything. "I don't know. Just give me time. Don't tell anybody else. We don't want Madison's parents figuring it out more than they probably already have. It reduces the whole thing to a complete farce."

"More than it already is?" Liam said, warning in his tone.

"What did you expect me to do? Her parents are horrible people." Aaron looked over at Lincoln. "Sorry. I know they're your aunt and uncle. But, seriously."

"I hate them. Really hate them. I don't even know if they're going to be invited to our wedding," Lincoln replied.

Ethan spoke up. "Holland and I already decided they aren't. Her family's not going to be invited, either. It's pretty much just going to be a huge Montgomery family wedding. Fuck the rest of your families. I'm sorry, but I'm putting my foot down here."

Lincoln shook his head and smiled before leaning down and kissing Ethan on the lips.

Ronin propped himself against the railing next to Aaron, wincing as he adjusted his prosthesis. He was working with an updated version from what Aaron could remember and looked to be having some problems. He'd been through hell and back, but he never complained. It made Aaron's issues feel small in comparison.

"Madison's family sounds like a bunch of assholes," Ronin began and then winced for an entirely different reason, glancing at Lincoln. "Sorry."

"Don't be. My aunt and uncle are assholes," Lincoln said with a laugh. "Seriously, you don't have to clarify you're talking about her parents only. I'm pretty much an asshole for not wanting to be part of the family. And for walking away from the situation. I try to shield Madison as much as I can, but she still loves them for some goddamn reason," Lincoln grumbled into his beer. Ethan leaned over and kissed him on the cheek.

Ethan gave Lincoln a sad smile. "She loves them because they're her parents. I remember a time when they were nicer than they are now."

"I just want to shake them for doing what they did." Aaron told the guys everything that had happened during the dinner, including them inviting Guy. Everyone just stared before they all started grumbling and shouting at once.

"My God," Benjamin said. "I'm surprised you didn't punch the woman. Not that you'd ever hit a female, but I feel like this would have been an appropriate time."

Aaron snorted at his cousin. "Oh, I thought about it,

believe me. But I stormed away angrily, wasn't polite, and drove to a park with Madison so I could yell at her. I was very mature."

"You yelled at my baby cousin?" Lincoln asked, glowering.

Aaron held up his hands, keeping his beer secure.

"Yes. But she yelled back, and we just talked..." He trailed off a bit, and Lincoln narrowed his eyes.

Ronin snorted from behind him, while everyone else started to laugh.

"Talk. Sure. Just talking? What's going on with you and my cousin?" Lincoln asked.

"Nothing," Aaron lied quickly. "I'm just her fake fiancé. Everything's normal."

"Nothing is normal about the sentence you just said," Ronin said, laughing. "I need to tell my girlfriend. At least when this is all over, and I'm allowed to tell her."

"Hey, did you know that Ronin is dating my coworker, Julia?" Ethan asked, helping Aaron change the subject with a wink.

"Seriously? Small town," Aaron said, grateful.

"Yeah, we've been together for a while," Ronin said, shrugging. "We didn't realize that we knew the same family until we talked about the Montgomerys one night. You guys breed more than rabbits," Ronin said, and the rest of them laughed.

"And you haven't even met my siblings yet," Benjamin said. "I have four of them."

"Dear God. There's like a hundred of you."

Aaron set down his beer and began counting on his fingers, laughing. "Yeah, maybe a hundred and twenty by now. They all keep breeding, too."

Ronin snorted. "I'm glad I was invited to this then without having to marry into the family. Unless that's somehow on the table for later."

"Since you're my friend now," Marcus began, "you're one of them."

"If somebody does the *one of us* cult chant, I'm going to walk away," Ronin snarled as Aaron opened his mouth to say that exact thing, apparently at the same time as Ethan. Both of them threw back their heads and laughed while the others joined in.

"We have this cult conversation often," Ethan began. "But we're not a cult or in a cult. We're just a family that wants the best for everybody involved. And right now, that includes having some ribs. Because I am starving, and they smell amazing. Liam, are you watching the ribs, or are we going to end up eating charcoal?"

Liam flipped him off and went over to the smoker.

"They're almost ready. I also made coleslaw, potato salad, regular salad, beans, mac and cheese, corn, and a few other things. I even brought Arden's cornbread, and I might die just thinking about it. It smells so good."

"What do you mean? We have veggies?" Aaron asked. "I thought this was a man's evening."

"Men can eat vegetables," Benjamin said, narrowing his eyes even though there was laughter in them. "It's this wonderful thing. If we eat healthy food, it means we can eat more. And we don't die of cardiovascular disease at the age of forty. I mean, we all know that Liam here is nearing that age."

"Fuck you. Seriously. Fuck you hard. That's just mean," Liam said.

"Didn't we all make fun of him when he was turning thirty before all of us?" Aaron asked, feeling lighter than he had in days.

"Yes. And that's what makes this fun," Benjamin said, grinning. "He will always reach milestones before us. We can either envy him for certain ones or take pride in knowing that we can make fun of him."

"I'm your elder, you're supposed to respect me," Liam said, sounding as stern as he could, even though he was laughing.

"Sure. Whatever you say," Ronin said, looking at the ribs and the smoker.

"You know, the way these ribs are placed reminds me of that *Criminal Minds* episode that just aired."

Aaron snapped his fingers and nodded. "I was just thinking that. That cult where they were eating the remains of others? It was kind of gross, but they came up with their signature barbecue sauce and were selling it nationwide."

"Why would you bring that up?" Lincoln asked.

"Seriously?" Ethan asked. "We're about to eat, and you're talking about human remains and selling barbecue sauce? Oh God, Marcus, you brought another *Criminal Minds* junkie into our family?"

"At least you didn't say *cult*," Ronin said, and they all burst out laughing, even as they all shuddered.

"Now I don't know if I want to eat these ribs," Marcus said. "That sort of ruined the moment."

"I'm sure if we keep drinking beer and start on the chicken first, it'll be okay," Benjamin said, even though he sounded doubtful.

"And, once again, a discussion of cannibalism and *Criminal Minds* has ruined a meal," Aaron said deadpan. The rest of them threw napkins and paper plates at him, and he ducked, laughing.

He honestly had no idea what he was going to do about Madison. He sure as fuck wasn't going to talk about the kiss or whatever they were going to do with and for each other later. For now, he would laugh and try to remember that he was doing this to make her happy and not because he wanted her taste again.

The fact that he craved her? That was just a bonus.

At least, that's what he told himself.

CHAPTER EIGHT

Madison was not getting ready for a date. She was getting ready for her fake date. Did that mean she was fake getting ready?

She ran her hands over her newly clean face and groaned. She was making things far too complicated, and it was only getting worse. The fact that it could *get* worse worried her, considering how far off the deep end she had already gone when it came to Aaron fricking Montgomery.

She should not have agreed to this. She shouldn't have agreed to any of it. But she couldn't help it when she was in the moment. Everything he said had made sense. Now, here she was, about to go on a practice and public date so others spying for her mother would know that they were out and about and not just pretending. The fact that they were actually playing a part notwithstanding.

She and Aaron had decided that they should go out for dinner and then maybe a walk in the moonlight later. And they'd do it in a park that many people frequented after dates so others would see them together. Madison had a feeling that they were just using the fakeness as an excuse, and she honestly wasn't sure how she felt about that. All she knew was that she had agreed to it, and she was pretty sure that some of it had been her idea.

She was going on a date with Aaron Montgomery. It could be that nobody would witness it, that nobody they knew or anybody her mother knew would see. It might be for nothing.

Or, it might end up being an actual date.

"It's not," she told herself and looked at her reflection in the mirror before putting on her moisturizer and beginning her makeup routine.

She loved playing with makeup and had a new friend that did it for a living, so she'd learned a few tricks from her YouTube channel.

Zia was far better than Madison could ever hope to be. Still, she thought she did a decent job with concealer and eyeshadow. She didn't look too overdone, but she felt happy and pretty. She always did her makeup for work because she wanted to, not because she felt like she had to. Most of the time, she ended up with nothing but lip balm on her lips. But that was because she worked at a bakery in a coffee shop, and when she was in the back, she just couldn't deal with melting cosmetics.

She quickly changed into her dress for the evening, one that flared at the hips and made her feel like a fairy princess going out dancing. It had a thin layer of tulle under the main fabric, and it made her feel as if she were dancing in the clouds as she pranced about.

It might be ridiculous for some people to wear, but it made her feel pretty. And tonight, she was going out on a date—or rather a *fake date*—with Aaron freaking Montgomery. So, she was going to wear what she wanted.

Maybe she should change into jeans and look casual. Or sweats. He'd seen her in sweats before. She could wear sweats.

She needed to stop thinking the word *sweats*. Because now she was sweating just thinking about it.

She slid her feet into her heels, put on her jewelry and perfume, and wondered if she had been wrong putting on her sexy underwear. It was a lace thong panty set, a beautiful peach color that matched her outfit, and not something that she wore all the time. She loved wearing lace and silk, but she also liked wearing cotton underwear that covered her entire ass.

The fact that she wasn't wearing those tonight spoke of her subconscious wondering if somebody might see what she wore under her dress. That would not be happening. Just because she and Aaron had kissed and might be kissing again later and we're going on a date, didn't mean that anybody would see her underwear but her.

What if she was in a car accident and they had to take off her dress to save her? Did she need to have cute underwear for that?

Maybe not sexy underwear that made her feel like a goddess. Now she was thinking far too hard. Everything was fine. Aaron wasn't going to see her underwear, but the idea that she was wearing it in front of him? It made her feel...powerful.

Or that she was losing her mind. Either way.

I'm only doing this for myself.

She repeated that mantra as the doorbell rang. She froze, wondering if Aaron was a good forty-five minutes early for their date. Madison might be ready, but that didn't matter. She needed the time to calm down and focus.

Her hands shook, and she didn't know why.

Tonight was just two friends pretending to be engaged. Nothing more, nothing less. And a complete lie.

She opened the door, and an odd mix of relief and disappointment filled her.

Bristol stood there with another woman that looked similar to her.

"You look amazing," Bristol said, clapping her hands. "We're too late to help you get ready, sorry."

"That's totally my fault," the stranger said. "Traffic was horrible getting over to Boulder, but I'm here now. And you do look amazing, Madison."

Madison blinked a few times. "I'm sorry, but who are you? And why are you here, Bristol? Not that I don't love you, but I'm confused."

"I'm so sorry. I seem to have started in the middle of a conversation. This is my cousin, Annabelle. Since her brother came over to Boulder last weekend to hang out with the guys, she decided to come tonight to hang out with me. I'm very blessed. And *I* am here because I like to help my friends get ready for dates. Especially first dates that can be scary or weird. But it seems you're ready to go. You really do look amazing. Your makeup is on point."

Madison just blinked, and somehow found herself taking a step back so the two Montgomery women could walk into the house.

"I'd offer you guys something to drink, but Aaron's going to be here soon." She paused. "Actually, he's going to be here in forty-five minutes. I'm done and ready to go way too early. So, how about I get you something to drink?"

"What do you have?" Annabelle asked, her eyes bright and kind.

"I just made fresh lemonade. From actual lemons."

"The only way to make it," Bristol said. "Not that I actually make lemonade on my own. That takes a lot of work and energy, and I'm not good at it. I always end up making it either too tart or too sweet. But yes, yes, yes, yes, lemonade."

They made their way to the kitchen. When Madison went to open her fridge, Bristol leaned forward and grabbed the lemonade.

"Glasses are on the top right shelf," Bristol said, and Madison just stood there blinking.

"We don't want you to get anything on your dress. We're here to comfort you in your time of need. Or to annoy you, whatever you want to call it," Bristol explained.

"You are pushy, but in a nice way," Madison corrected.

Annabelle threw her head back and laughed, and Bristol flipped her cousin off.

"I am. Did you hear what happened to Arden?"

"Something new?" Madison asked, worried about the other woman. Arden had lupus and was going through a good spell, but Madison knew from Arden's previous experiences that it didn't always last.

"No, I'm sorry. She's doing great. I meant what happened the first time I met her," Bristol said quickly, her hands raised as she set the pitcher of lemonade down on the counter. "I didn't mean to worry you."

"Don't do that." Madison let out a breath, nervous for so many reasons.

"I'm sorry," Bristol said again.

"Arden is great," Annabelle said into the silence. "We had dinner when she came to visit my side of the family up in Fort Collins."

"I forgot about that," Bristol said. "I'm glad you met her."

"I'm sure we'll meet up again. We're all trying to do better about seeing each other," Annabelle said. There was something in her tone that made Bristol meet her gaze and share a look that Madison didn't understand.

Something was going on with those Montgomerys. She had always thought they got along great, all sets of the cousins. But maybe she was wrong. Or perhaps she was trying to see too much into it. She *was* nervous about her date—or rather, her fake date—with Aaron.

"What did you do with Arden?" Annabelle asked.

"I went over to her house even though I had never met her before to help her get ready for her first date with Liam. I didn't illegally get her address, but it was close."

Annabelle threw back her head and laughed again, a happy sound that reminded Madison of angels and bells. She just shook her head.

"I heard about that. I'm shocked that Arden didn't slam and lock the door, never to see a Montgomery again."

"Well, we are tenacious," Bristol said. "In retrospect, as soon as I knocked on the door, I realized I had made a terrible mistake. Not everybody finds me as sweet and kind and caring as I think in my head. We were fortunate that Arden let me into her life after I surprised her."

"Yes, you are fortunate. Because I think Liam murdering you would have put a damper on the whole family thing."

"You're right. But alas, their romance persisted, and they're doing fantastic. Speaking of romance, are you ready for tonight?"

Madison shook her head. "It's not real." She turned to Annabelle. "I mean..."

Crap. She sucked at this lying thing.

Unless she was lying to herself.

Annabelle held up her hands. "We know. At least Benjamin and I know."

Madison relaxed. "Thank you. And I appreciate you guys coming over, but I'm okay. I'm only going out to dinner and probably for a walk with Aaron. We're just hanging out."

"As an engaged couple," Annabelle said softly.

"Fake engaged couple," Madison corrected.

"That's fine. Whatever," Bristol said, holding up her hands. "First off, this lemonade is amazing. I'm jealous that I can't make this. The next time we have a family barbecue or something, you need to bring this over. Marcus loves lemonade."

That made Madison smile. "Okay, I can make that happen."

"Good. Second, have fun tonight. You look wonderful. We came to give you a pep talk, but you look ready to go."

"But I finally got to meet you," Annabelle said, grinning.

"I'm glad that we got to meet, as well," Madison said. "So, if I remember right, you have four other siblings?"

"Yes, I have a twin named Archer, another set of

twins named Beckett and Benjamin, and a little sister named Paige."

Madison's eyes widened. "I'm never going to be able to remember all of that."

"There's no reason you should." Annabelle laughed. "Unless you *do* marry Aaron, and then there will be a quiz once you're indoctrinated into the Montgomerys."

That made Madison's eyes widen. "There's a quiz?"

Bristol laughed. "Yes, you have to take it once you enter middle school if you're born a Montgomery. But by then, there's usually a whole new generation. Or someone else has gotten married, and it just gets super complicated. We'll do an entire set of flashcards, and maybe a light show so you can get the names right."

"Good thing I'm not marrying Aaron, then."

"Good thing," Annabelle said, giving Bristol a look that Madison chose to ignore.

She did not need to remember all of the Montgomery cousins. She only needed to remember the ones that she currently knew because she was not marrying Aaron. Even if they *were* going on a maybe real date tonight.

The girls stayed for a little while longer and then headed out, complimenting Madison's look once more before leaving her alone and wondering how she had gotten into this situation. Thankfully, she didn't have to stew long because the doorbell rang again. She swallowed hard, wondering what she was going to say to him.

She needn't have worried, though. All thought left her when she saw Aaron standing there wearing gray slacks, a crisp shirt with the sleeves rolled up to his elbows, showing off his sexy-as-hell forearms, and a wicked grin.

"I saw Bristol driving away with my cousin in the front seat as I pulled into your neighborhood. Should I apologize?"

She shook her head, reaching around to grab her wristlet. "Please don't. I love Bristol. She's just...a lot sometimes."

"You know they say that about me, too."

There was an awkward moment, and then Aaron leaned forward and brushed a kiss across her lips.

She moaned, thankful that she was wearing matte lipstick instead of anything shiny that would spread.

"Hey there. You ready to go?" he asked, clearing his throat as he moved away.

"I think I am. Finally." She didn't know why she'd added that last part, but there was no taking it back now. Aaron searched her face, and she had to remind herself that this wasn't real. It couldn't be.

"So, pasta?" she asked, wondering if she could say anything more ridiculous.

He smiled at her, and for some reason, she wanted this night to be real. Yes, he'd kissed her. Sure, the kiss had felt real. But they were only playing. It was all an act.

Still, she couldn't think clearly.

"Yes. Pasta. You know we could go for salads or something light and airy, but I want the amount of carbs that will make me roll out of there."

"I have been craving pasta for a week. So, no, I am not getting a freaking salad."

"That's my girl," he said, squeezing her hand.

She tried not to think that it was real because it hurt to do so.

They talked about their days, about the café and his art, and she leaned into the seat as she listened to him speak. He had a deep, soothing voice that sometimes rumbled a bit if he got tired, but he wasn't as growly as his brothers. He surely wasn't as gruff as her cousin. He seemed to love life a bit more. Or maybe he was just happier. The fact that he was doing this for her meant that he had a secure sense of self that she couldn't even hope to possess.

She truly appreciated him and everything he was doing. Though she wasn't sure how to tell him.

They sat down in an angled corner booth, one with leather backs taller than her head. She just sank in, grinning.

"They don't make booths like these anymore."

"No. And I don't like sitting in the middle of the area either, feeling like I'm on display." Aaron winced. "Though I think that's what we're supposed to do tonight."

Madison tried to ignore the hurt that statement caused because it was true. She shouldn't feel bad about it.

"We can always take a picture and post it on social media. That's what couples do, right?"

"It's been so long that I don't even remember anymore. Well, we can do that."

Aaron pulled out his phone and turned it to face them. Then he wrapped his arm around her shoulders before kissing her cheek and hitting the side button. She saw her face in the photo, her eyes wide, surprise evident, and Aaron chuckled.

"Don't look so surprised, it's supposed to be real."

"Yeah, sure."

He took another photo, and she grinned, happiness in her eyes. She hoped that nobody saw the fear there, too. The disappointment.

Because she knew it was there and could definitely see it.

Clear as day.

Or maybe she was projecting.

The waiter came, and Aaron put away his phone after posting on Instagram. They ordered appetizers and their meals and a bottle of wine to share.

Madison would be stuffed, and she could not wait.

"They have the best salads. The lettuce is perfectly cold and crisp."

"I thought you said you didn't want a salad?" Aaron teased.

"I'm eating the salad. As well as the olives and the red onions. I'm sorry, but I have to eat the red onions."

He laughed. "I am, too. So, if we both have onion breath, it's not a big turn-off." He winked, and she didn't know if it was for show just in case somebody was around, or if it was real. It couldn't be real.

This was fake. It was all a lie.

They were sipping their wine and nibbling on breadsticks when someone cleared their throat from the edge of the table. Madison looked up, pulling her gaze away from Aaron, and blinked. How the hell was this happening?

"Madison."

"Guy? What are you doing here?" she asked,

knowing she sounded rude, but this was a little ridiculous.

"I'm here to meet some clients for a drink. I saw you sitting over here, looking lovely, and I had to see you and say hello. After all, your mother wouldn't want me to stay away."

"Guy," Aaron growled, this time a true snarl. Madison hadn't heard that tone from him before. And she didn't know why she liked it so much.

It sent shivers down her spine, but she focused on Guy, trying not to lose her mind that he was here. But wasn't this what they wanted? He would report back to her mom, and Mother would know that she and Aaron were together.

Why did this feel tainted, then? Like Guy had ruined everything.

"As you can see, we're busy," Madison said, trying to keep her voice sweet. She didn't know what else to say. "Please give my mother my best," she said pointedly. Guy raised a brow.

"I'm sure I'll be seeing you soon." Guy winked and walked away, leaving her feeling disturbed.

"I hate him," Aaron growled.

"I'm not a big fan right now either. I'm sorry."

"Don't you dare apologize. We are about to eat some delicious red onions and the rest of the meal.

Enjoy yourself." He leaned forward and smacked a kiss on her lips, and she groaned, unable to hold it back.

He grinned, tucking her hair behind her ear.

"I like that sound."

She swallowed hard.

"Oh?"

"Yeah. I'm enjoying tonight, Madison. Just you and me. Is that okay?"

"You and me."

It wasn't just them. This was a lie, just like everything else. But she could pretend. She could just be. When she kissed Aaron again, ignoring the salads that had been placed in front of them, she could only lean her head against him and pretend.

Because as much as she wanted this to be real, it wasn't. It couldn't be. However, she always had her dreams.

Even if the taste of him was still on her lips.

CHAPTER NINE

Aaron stood in Madison's living room, the scent of coffee filling the air, and anticipation sliding through both of them. At least through him. Though he wanted to imagine that it was for her, as well.

Why was he here? Why hadn't he just dropped her off, called it a night, and walked away?

It didn't matter, he hadn't. And, honestly, he didn't want to.

Madison walked out, two mugs of coffee in her hands, her heels off, and her dress clinging to her curves in the most sensual way possible. He had to swallow hard so he didn't reach out, take those mugs from her, and ravish her on the floor.

Yes, ravish. Those were the words sliding through Aaron's head right then.

Ravish, fuck, make love to, have sex with, plunder... every random connotation he could think of filled his mind. All he wanted to do was touch her. He needed her. Had to taste her.

Once again, he knew it was a mistake, but he didn't care.

Madison handed over the cup of coffee, and he wrapped his hand around the mug, letting the heat seep into his skin. "Thank you."

She smiled at him. He liked that smile, it seemed real if a bit nervous. He hated that they were doing this because of what her mother was doing to her, but he had to be honest with himself and say that he liked it regardless. Not the fact that Madison had been hurt, but the idea that they could spend time together. He knew it wasn't smart to allow his cravings to turn into wants and needs, but he couldn't hold back now.

Even though he knew he should.

He still had the taste of her on his lips from after dinner.

He could barely remember anything they'd eaten, even though he knew the food was delicious. All he could do was remember the taste of her, her feel, and her scent.

Maybe he was losing his mind. Perhaps he should walk away. But he wasn't going to. Instead, he took a sip of his coffee, his gaze never leaving hers.

"Dinner was nice," Madison said after a minute, most likely to fill the silence. He was glad that she'd spoken first because he didn't know what to say.

So unlike him.

"It was great. Although I could have done without Guy being there." He hadn't meant to say that, but now that it was out there, he really regretted it. When Madison winced, he spoke up. "Sorry, let's not bring him up. Ever."

"No, let's talk about him for a second. And then never bring him up again." She winked as she said it, and he was glad for that.

"What do you want to say about him?"

Why did he sound so grumpy?

"I don't know why he was there. It could be a coincidence. It is a nice place, and he did have a drink with someone. It looked to be work-related as he said. *Or* my mother could have someone on the payroll watching me, following me, and she sent Guy there to ruin our date."

Aaron blinked a couple of times and shook his head. "You know, I would say you might be overreaching because it sounds like something I read in a book once.

But the more I learn about your parents, the more I think that actually could happen."

"Right? It's a little worrying. However, either way, we both know that my mother will hear that we were out on a date. And that we were kissing and all that." She said the last part quickly, and Aaron took another sip of his coffee, the warmth suffusing him before he set the cup down on the table next to him. Then he took hers, as well.

"I'm going to do something just to try it out. Will you let me?"

Curiosity filled her gaze, and he swallowed hard.

"I should say no. We should both say no."

"But we're not going to. Are we?"

"So, this is where I say no?" she asked. He stepped forward, her body right in front of his, the heat of her a caress on his skin. He cupped her face.

"Do you trust me?" he asked.

"Of course, I do. I wouldn't be here if I didn't."

Then he lowered his head and brushed his lips against hers.

She moaned, wrapping her arms around him, her hands moving up and down his back.

He smiled against her lips before arching her neck slightly, deepening the kiss. He needed her taste, needed her groans and moans.

He pushed his hands through her hair, tugging slightly on the pink and blond strands so they moved from her face, and he could angle her the way he wanted.

She sent a shocked gasp into his mouth as he tugged a little harder. He pulled away, panting, looking down at her face.

"Too much?" he asked, worried.

"No. I don't know. What are we doing?" she asked, her voice breathy.

"Anything we want."

"I thought this wasn't supposed to be real. If we keep doing this with no one watching, then it's real."

A smile crept over Aaron's face. "If we do this while people are watching, we might end up in jail," he said with a laugh.

Her skin turned a pretty pink that matched her hair. He kissed her again.

"This is just us. You and me, like I said."

"We're fake engaged, but not fake anything else?" she asked.

"That works for me." And then he stopped that line of conversation with a kiss, afraid that if they kept discussing it, they would talk themselves out of what they were doing.

The whole situation was too fraught with mistakes

and potholes that could ruin everything. So, they wouldn't talk about it.

He kept kissing her before letting his hands roam down her curves, over her hips. He squeezed them, and she arched towards him, his dick pressing into her stomach.

They both groaned, and then he pulled away, needing air.

"You trust me?" he asked again.

"I already said... Of course, I do." She narrowed her eyes, a smile playing on her lips.

"What exactly have you been reading in those romance books of yours?"

He grinned then before throwing his head back and laughing.

"A lot of kinky shit that you're probably not going to want on a first date," he said, laughing some more.

"I've read the same books as you, thank you very much. Which book are we talking about?"

He named one that he knew they had both read, even though it wasn't the most popular one.

Her eyes widened, and she smiled. "Well, I think some of that could be fun. But we remain friends, right? Because that's what we need. Friends first. Always."

He nodded solemnly before kissing her again. "Friends always," he whispered before reaching down and sliding his hands under her dress to grab her ass. He lifted her into the air.

She squealed and wrapped her legs around his waist before he latched his mouth to hers again, kissing her while carrying her towards the back of the house.

"I take it your bedroom's this way?"

"Yes, but we could have done it in the living room, too."

"I think I'm going to need a little more space for what I have planned."

"Oh," she whispered.

And then they were in the bedroom, and he slowly let her down, her body pressing against his in a sensual rub as she kept kissing him.

His heart raced, and all he wanted to do was keep touching her, needing her. But he wanted to have some fun first. And he knew that she did, too. They could both use a little fun with what they were doing.

He slowly reached around, undid the tie on the neck of her dress, and unzipped the back. All the while, his gaze never left hers.

"You're pretty good at that," she breathed.

"I'm just learning from you," he whispered, smiling.

"You're not going to say that you've had lots of practice?" she said with a laugh.

In answer, he kissed her hard again, and then her

dress hit the floor. She stood there in a lacy thong and bra that allowed him to see her nipples.

He groaned, took a staggering step back, and clutched his chest over his heart.

"You're killing me here. You had that on for the entire night?"

She blushed all the way to those pretty nipples. "What? I wanted to feel pretty."

"Just for yourself? Or for me?" he asked, not knowing if he really wanted the answer.

"I lied when I told myself that it was only for me."

"Good answer."

And then he was on her again, kissing and needing.

She helped him with his shirt, and then his belt and pants. Soon, he was standing there in his boxer briefs, running his hands up and down her body.

When he wasn't sure he could handle anymore, she squeezed his dick over the cotton of his shorts. He groaned and led her to the bed.

He picked her up and placed her softly in the middle, grinning as she laughed at him, trailing her fingers over his skin.

She lay spread out before him, and he reached down to gently rub his thumb over her nipple that peeked through the lace.

"Beautiful," he rasped.

"You keep touching me like that, and I'm not going to last long."

He smiled. "I thought that was my line." He lowered his head and gently sucked on her nipple through the lace of her bra. She arched into him, moaning, and he let his hand trail down her belly, the soft skin tantalizing underneath his palm before he cupped her.

"Aaron," she whispered.

He slowly patted her core, using the lace's friction before tugging the material to the side and gently probing her entrance.

"Already wet," he whispered.

"Well, that's all your fault."

He winked before kissing her again.

"Good." And then he inched his finger in slowly, curling it as she tightened around him.

She moaned again, and he went back to feasting on her nipples, tugging the lace down to gain better access to her sweet skin. He added a second finger, and then a third, working her hard as she arched, her hips practically coming off the mattress. When he moved, hard and fast, she finally came on him, her thighs clamping around his wrist. He grinned against her breasts before capturing her mouth and the shocked moan she let free.

He slowly removed his fingers, then met her gaze

before licking her juices off, slowly, knowing the taste would haunt him until the end of his days.

So sweet, so fucking tempting.

"I can't believe you just did that," she said, blushing.

"I'm not done yet."

He kissed her again, knowing that she could likely taste herself on his lips before he got up and winked. "Be right back."

"You're leaving me like this?" she asked.

"Yes, I am. But I promise I'll be right back."

He practically ran to the kitchen, his dick hard and caged within his boxer briefs. He was grateful for that. If he weren't covered, he'd probably have hurt himself with how quickly he moved.

He got a bowl, filled it with ice, and found a linen napkin perfectly ironed in her drawer. He returned to the bedroom and held back a laugh as she sat up on the bed, narrowing her eyes at him.

"You got ice?" she asked, her voice a little sharp.

"You'll see."

He set the items down on the end of the bed and gently prowled towards her, kissing her hard and tugging on her hair.

"You said you trusted me."

"And you left me after you gave me an orgasm. That's not very nice."

"I promise I'll give you another."

He kissed her again before moving her to her back.

He reached around for the linen napkin and raised a brow.

"You're going to tie me up?"

"No, not today."

He kissed her again and gently tied the napkin around her eyes.

Her breath caught, her lips parting, so he kissed her again, knowing that she couldn't see him.

"Too tight?"

"No. I kind of like it."

"Anything you don't like, you tell me."

"Promise."

He undid her bra, her breasts falling into his palms. He licked and sucked them, loving the way she squirmed beneath him.

When he reached for the bowl, he pulled out an ice cube and let the cool droplets of water fall onto her breasts.

She gasped, and he grinned before tracing her nipple with the ice cube, loving the way she puckered. It made him impossibly hard. He blew cool air over her pebbled flesh before licking and sucking, bringing her buds to such hard points that he knew she was aching for him.

She squirmed, reached for him. He let her. He wasn't going to restrain her, not really. That wasn't what he wanted. He wanted her to touch him. Wanted her to lead the way. He just wanted to play. And he knew she did, as well.

When he tugged off her panties, she helped him by raising her butt. Immediately, he was between her legs, her pussy right in front of his face. But before he licked, he gently pressed an ice cube to her clit.

Her hips shot off the bed, and he moved back, laughing before he latched his mouth to her pussy, licking and sucking.

"Aaron!"

He kept licking, alternating between his mouth and the ice cube, to the point where he knew that she was going to come hard and fast.

But this was fun. As long as she was smiling and laughing with him, and probably groaning in frustration a bit, he'd continue to do this. Anything she wanted. That was why he was here, after all. Wasn't it?

Because he would do anything for her.

He pushed those thoughts from his mind, afraid of the journey they'd take him on, and kept playing with her, alternating between the ice and the heat of his mouth.

When she came again, he lapped up her juices before leaning back and setting the bowl on the floor and tugging off his boxer briefs. He put his feet down and reached over to undo the napkin tied over her eyes.

She blinked up at him, her eyes dark with need, and licked her lips. Her gaze went straight to his dick, and he swore it twitched at the attention.

"Can you come closer?"

"If I do, I'm going to come in your mouth, and that's not where I want to finish."

She winked. "Just a little taste?"

"Well, how can I deny you?"

He put the condom that he had pulled out of his pants earlier on the pillow next to her head, and she gave it a nod before he kneeled in front of her face. She reached for him. The first touch of her soft hand on his dick almost made him come immediately, but he gritted his teeth and held back.

She pumped him a couple of times before she moved to her side and swallowed him whole.

He slid his hand through her hair, let his head fall back, and groaned.

"Dear God."

She hummed on him, hollowing her mouth and

throat so she could take him deeper, bobbing a bit, just enough to make him want to thrust. But he didn't. He wanted her to be the one in control this time.

When his balls tightened, and he almost came, he pulled away, gasping, and reached for the condom.

"I need to be inside you."

"Same. I need you."

He retook her lips, then rolled the condom over his length before positioning them on the bed so he was on his back, and she hovered over him.

"Ride me."

"Anything you want, Aaron. Although, I thought you were supposed to be the one taking control today."

"We're not in a book. It's just you and me," he said. "This is for you. You're the one center stage. You get me?"

Some emotion crossed her face, and he was afraid that he had said the wrong thing. He didn't know where the words had come from, but they were out there now, and there was no taking them back.

"I like that. And, yes, it's just you and me."

And then she sank onto him, and he was lost.

He gripped her hips with bruising intensity and forced himself not to thrust into her. She leaned forward, her breasts swinging above his face as she shook.

"You're so fucking big. Give me a second."

"Take all the time you need," he murmured before lapping at her nipples in front of him.

And then he spread her cheeks. When she was ready, he pumped into her hard. There was no need to go slow, no need to take it an inch at a time.

Because they both needed this.

He spread her with one hand, then let his other hand move up her back to tug on her hair. He needed her at the perfect angle to get her neck, her breasts, her mouth.

She met him thrust for thrust, and when his balls tightened, and he came, she climaxed with him, both of them moaning into each other's mouths, sweat-slick and finally nearly sated.

He rolled to the side, still deep inside her, and kept kissing, kept touching.

"That might've been the best fake sex I've ever had," she whispered.

He laughed, still buried balls-deep. Then he held her close, just needing to touch her. Afraid what would happen if he didn't.

So damn afraid.

"There was nothing fake about that. There better not have been." He gave her ass a sharp slap, and she laughed again, kissing him hard once more.

"Nothing fake about that." A look of fear crawled over her face again. It was the same trepidation he had.

They were going into uncharted territory here. Down a path that could hurt them both.

But he ignored it and knew that she needed to ignore it, as well. Then he kissed her again before slowly moving in and out of her, just a bit. They could have fakeness and unreality in what their promises were to each other for the outside world. But right here, right now, this was real.

So real, it scared him.

But he wasn't going to think about that. Wouldn't let himself believe.

This was just for tonight. And maybe tomorrow. When she needed him to walk away, he would.

He just didn't know who he would be when he did.

CHAPTER TEN

Madison's hips swayed to the music as she focused on her task, the cupcakes in front of her tantalizing, the frosting smelling of strawberry and cream cheese. Her decadent double chocolate fudge cupcakes with strawberry cream cheese frosting were a hit, and one that she could dive into. So, she wouldn't. If she did, she'd end up with a toothache because she couldn't stop at just one.

But maybe she'd eat a spoonful of frosting. Or a bowl full. Okay, perhaps not that much.

She focused on the frosting and the song playing through her headphones, humming softly to herself as she worked.

Brynn was up front with her other two staff

members, each working on coffee and busing tables, and helping the overall atmosphere of Sin in a Cup.

Madison loved this job, adored the people she worked with.

The only thing that ever dampened her elation was the fact that she could hear her mother calling it nothing and using rude names for her place of business, the people she worked with, and criticizing her weight.

But she pushed those things out of her mind because she had far more important stuff to think about.

Like Aaron.

No, not him. Today, she was only focusing on her cupcakes. That was it—nothing more, nothing less.

She loaded up the last set and started her frosting again, trying not to think about the blush that covered her cheeks at the thought of Aaron.

She'd had sex before.

Phenomenally great sex.

She and her last boyfriend had even done most of the things that she and Aaron had done. She liked things on the kinkier side, yet she also enjoyed things sweet, happy, and playful.

Somehow, Aaron had mixed all of that together to create a night of perfect bliss that scared her.

Because even if she had done each of those things

individually before with another person, it hadn't been the same as it was with Aaron.

And that scared her even more. It should because she hadn't expected him.

He had been on the periphery of her life for years. Lincoln and Ethan had been best friends for as long as Madison could remember. Honestly, she couldn't think of a time when the Montgomerys hadn't been part of her life. When Lincoln wanted to pull her away from her parents a bit more and bring her into his life as much as possible, she had become an honorary Montgomery of sorts. She'd embraced them as much as they embraced her. She knew some of their family secrets, knew their hurts and their likes and dislikes. Just like they knew some of hers.

And Aaron had always been there. The one she laughed with, the one she joked around with.

But she had never let herself think of him as anything more than that. He was Ethan's baby brother. The one who talked fast, though not as quickly as Ethan. The one who loved *Criminal Minds* and whose favorite author of all time was Lisa Kleypas. He was the one who always did his best to make sure his siblings were happy, sometimes forgetting to do the same for himself.

She had noticed all of this from the sidelines, and

though the Montgomerys had tried their best to pull her from that place, she had always known where she was most comfortable.

And yet, here she was, no longer on the sidelines when it came to Aaron.

She was someone who needed labels, who needed firm examples and boxes to put everybody and everything in. It was the only way she could focus on what she needed to do with the rest of her life. She had a home she loved, a job she adored, and she worked hard to keep both the way she wanted them. There had been many sleepless nights when it came to making her dreams come true. And while finding love had always been on her agenda, it had never truly happened.

Maybe her relationship with her family was part of that. But it was also her. She hadn't found what she wanted.

She wasn't saying that she loved Aaron. She didn't. She wasn't ready for that. She knew that once their fake relationship or whatever they were calling it ended, she would have to learn how to walk away yet still keep him in her life. Somehow, she'd become part of his family through Lincoln. They'd welcomed her with open arms and treated her far better than most of her own flesh and blood. Once this sham with Aaron ended, she wasn't sure how she would be able to face them...or him. She'd have to leave completely. Break all ties.

Leaving her a shattered mess of someone who didn't know their place.

She needed those labels, and she didn't know what she and Aaron were now. Were they fake engaged? Were they together for real?

Or were they somehow seeing each other casually while she wore his ring?

Finished with the cupcakes, she set down her piping bag and reached under her shirt for the ring that hung on the chain.

She swallowed hard and looked down at the diamond, admiring how it sparkled, almost as if mocking her. She tried to breathe, only she couldn't quite catch her breath.

She was engaged.

Yet it wasn't real.

She didn't know if what she had shared with Aaron in bed was real. It had felt real, the feel of him, the taste of him, his touch.

But what if nothing else was real?

He had said, "just you and me," and she had agreed. But that wasn't a label. That wasn't what she needed. The problem was, she had no idea *what* she needed. So, asking for a label would likely only end up in an explosion of nothingness with her hurt. Or worse, she would hurt him. He was a nice guy, only trying to help. The idea that she would end up hurting him because of her insecurities scared her more than anything. She would willingly walk alone and into the fire of her mother's wrath if it meant not hurting Aaron.

"Hey there. Are you done with those cupcakes?" Brynn asked as she hustled to the back. "People are already raving about them, and we just got a new order."

"This batch is ready," Madison said, shaking herself out of her reverie. She didn't always do the baking, but today she had wanted to throw herself into her cupcakes and do something routine like filling each cup with part of herself.

Brynn had seemed to understand that and took up the responsibilities up front with ease.

If Madison ever decided to open up a second branch someday, something she had been thinking about, perhaps in Fort Collins, she would definitely send Brynn out there to manage it if she were willing. It scared her to think of losing Brynn or even getting to a point where she was ready for the next phase of her job and career. But it was on her agenda and was something Brynn understood.

Things were changing, and yet Madison felt like she was drowning.

She hated it.

"You look sad, or maybe thoughtful. And you were playing with your ring again. Can I see it?" Brynn asked, coming closer.

Madison nodded, then went to wash her hands before taking the ring off and handing it to Brynn. Brynn oohed and aahed over the diamond and then smiled.

"Aaron has magnificent taste. And it's totally you. I just wish you could wear it on your hand more."

Madison looked down at her bare ring finger and wiggled it a bit. "Well, we don't want to lose it in a cupcake."

"Unless you're trying to set up a proposal. And then you don't put it in the batter, you set it on top of the frosting, so she doesn't swallow it and die."

"That's a morbid way to get engaged," Madison said with a laugh, taking back the ring when Brynn handed it over.

"Put it on and come up front. Some of your friends are here to see you."

Madison slid the ring onto her finger, wondering why it felt like it belonged there, and yet shouldn't be there all the same.

"My friends?"

"The Montgomerys, or the ones that are connected to the Montgomerys anyway. Another friend of theirs that I don't know yet is here, too. But I will meet them. Come on out. I'll work back here. You go do your magic up front."

Madison frowned and then took off her apron, making sure she didn't have flour or frosting anywhere.

Happy with her quick scan, she headed to the front and grinned at those seated at the table in the corner. Arden, Holland, Bristol, and another woman that Madison didn't recognize sat with smiles on their faces.

"Can you take a break?" Arden asked. Madison nodded.

"Yes, let me just grab something. Do you want anything?"

"Brynn took care of us. Come on. We've got a whole bunch of cupcakes."

That made Madison laugh, and she grabbed herself some water with cucumber then made her way to the table.

"Water and cucumber?" Bristol asked with a sigh. "I thought you would go for something sweet with lots of whipped cream."

"I might've eaten a lot of frosting in the back before

I came out here," Madison said honestly, and the girls laughed.

"Isn't that against code?" Holland teased, her eyes bright.

"I had a special frosting bowl in the break room, thank you very much. But please, yell that louder," she said with a laugh.

"I'm sorry, this is Ethan's friend Julia," Holland said. The other woman smiled and waved a bit. "Hi. I actually work with Ethan. And I'm also dating Marcus's friend, Ronin. If the already complicated situation wasn't enough."

Madison did the complicated math and snorted. "I've met Ronin, and I know Ethan and Marcus, so you're technically a Montgomery," Madison said quickly and froze as the girls gave her a look.

"I mean, you've been indoctrinated into the web or the cult or whatever. Oh! Clan's a good word," she said quickly, rambling.

"Yes, once you're friends with the family, apparently, you're one of them. I hear you're engaged to Aaron. Lovely ring. I guess you're really a Montgomery now, huh?"

Guilt swamped Madison, and she did her best not to look at the others. She knew they were aware that it was all fake, but Julia didn't. Madison hated lying, but the more people who knew it wasn't real, the harder it would be for her mother to leave it alone.

So, Madison just smiled. She had no idea what to say.

"Okay, tell me about these cupcakes," Arden said, licking her lips. "I already heard about the double chocolate with strawberry cream cheese frosting, but what else is there?"

"We have a lemon chiffon, a key lime, a birthday cake that has a bit of a champagne twist, and red velvet. Oh, and the carrot cake," Madison said, grateful she could change the subject quickly.

Thankfully, Julia didn't look as if anything were awkward.

"We just wanted to say hi and see how you were doing after your date," Bristol said, practically dancing in her seat.

"Really?" Madison asked. "You're going to be that blatant?"

"What do you mean? Your date?" Julia asked, looking truly confused.

The other women, however, helped her cover it up. Madison knew she couldn't keep this charade up for long. Not when she was already overcomplicating things when it came to Aaron.

"We like to get into each other's business. And

Bristol and our cousin were over at Madison's house earlier to help her get ready for her date with Aaron, much like Bristol likes to do for everybody."

Julia laughed. "I'm glad I'm already with Ronin, and we don't need to add a third to our relationship or anything. If we did, I bet Bristol would be there in a minute to help me date."

The way Julia said that made Madison raise a brow, while Julia blushed. The others didn't say anything.

There was a story there, but Madison was not going to touch it.

They moved on in their conversation, talking about their families and their jobs, thankfully not bringing up men again so Madison didn't have to continue lying to everybody and herself about what was going on between Aaron and her.

She left them at their table, needing to go back to work, when the door opened again. She held back a groan.

Guy strode through the door, looking suave and like a million bucks in a custom-tailored suit. Many gazes turned to him, and she did her best to look nonchalant. She didn't want to talk to him, and she had no idea what to say to him anyway.

"Madison, it's good to see you again."

"Since this is my shop, it's pretty much where you'll find me most days."

"Good to know," he said with a wink.

"Anyway, I need to get in the back and finish baking. Enjoy your day."

He reached out and grabbed her arm before she could move. She looked down at it, stunned that he would reach over the counter to touch her.

"I'm sorry," he said, sounding sincere as he let her go, his palm outstretched. "I wanted to talk to you. I didn't mean to startle you."

She knew the others were looking at them, and she didn't want to make a scene because that's what her family was good at. Since Guy was connected to her mother, apparently, he was good at it, as well.

"I'm working, Guy. But please enjoy a cupcake on me."

"You don't have to do that. But thank you. I might just have to taste one of your delectable sweets."

She did not groan at that horrible double entendre. It wasn't even clever.

"Enjoy."

"You should come out with me," he said.

She heard Brynn sputter beside her, and Madison let out a sigh. "I'm engaged," she lied, though it didn't feel like a lie as much as it had before. But that wasn't something she would be thinking about. "Please tell my mother you tried."

"This has nothing to do with your mother, Madison."

"It has everything to do with her. Goodbye, Guy," she said before walking to the back, not wanting to deal with him anymore.

She threw herself back into her work, grateful that he hadn't somehow found his way back to the kitchen.

She could not believe his audacity. She didn't know what her mother had on him or what she'd told him he would get out of marrying Madison, but she honestly didn't want any part of it. He might be attractive, they might have things in common, but he was creepy in her book. And the fact that he would go along with whatever her mother said? No, thanks.

She finished up her baking, then went back to her office to work on some paperwork. She already had a headache brewing for the day.

She looked down at her phone and saw that the girls had all texted in their group chat to see if she was okay.

She was surprised that they hadn't come to the back, but maybe Brynn had kept them from doing so. After all, nobody really wanted a scene, least of all her.

Madison: *I'm fine. Just working. Thank you so much for coming today. It was great to see you.*

Arden: *Are you okay for real?*

Bristol: *Do we need to hurt someone for you? Because we will. Or we'll send one of the guys.*

Holland: *We could totally do it ourselves, Bristol.*

Madison smiled.

Madison: *I'm fine. Really. It's just the guy that my mother tried to set me up with.*

She looked at the group chat name and was grateful it was only them and not Julia because that would have been another lie she'd have to deal with.

Arden: *We're setting up a girls' night, and you're coming. We can all talk about your date and everything else that you might not want to talk about. You're one of us now, even if you don't think so.*

Tears stung the backs of Madison's eyes. What could she say?

Bristol: *A nice girls' night, and I promise not to be annoying.*

Madison snorted.

Holland: *She'll do her best, haha.*

Bristol: *You know I'm sitting in the car next to you. I could hurt you, Holland.*

That made Madison laugh out loud.

Madison: *A girls' night sounds great. Be safe, and don't actually hurt each other.*

They all said their goodbyes, and she grinned, setting her phone down on her desk near her computer. When it rang, she picked it up without looking, wondering if it was one of them.

"Hello?"

"Madison. I cannot believe you threw Guy out like that. How could you?"

Madison groaned, knowing this was all her fault for not looking at the phone. She truly deserved this.

"Mother."

"Don't say *Mother* in that tone. I have a proposition for you."

"I'm still dealing with your last one," she said, tired. She pinched the bridge of her nose.

"Tone."

"You work on yours first," Madison said, proud of herself.

"The proposition, like I said. You'll come to your father's retreat at the lodge. No excuses. Bring Aaron. And if I approve, I'll call Guy off. But you better do well."

"Mom, no. I have a life. I have to work. Aaron has to work. We can't just drop everything and come to the lodge." She hated the lodge. It was always full of people who wanted something from her family, and therefore, tried to get it from her. She wasn't about to throw Aaron to those wolves. And she knew they would want him there. He was an up-and-coming artist, and his family was connected to certain circles that they would want to be a part of. No, she wouldn't do that.

"I don't care," her mom said.

"Mother."

"Do this, and we'll stop. We'll let you be. Do this now, or we'll never quit. We just want what's best for you."

Madison closed her eyes and counted to five, trying to breathe. She would have counted to ten, but she knew her mother would never let her have that time. At least it sounded like her mom that sometimes Maeve stepped over the line. Did Madison believe it would change anything?

She wasn't sure.

If Madison and Aaron pulled the whole fake engagement off, would her mother truly back off? Madison wanted to think so, but she didn't know for sure.

"Just this once," Madison said, hating herself. "If Aaron can take time away from his project, and if I can get Brynn and my staff to work my shifts, I will come."

"You're the boss, and he's an artist. You can both do whatever you need to."

"I'll do my best."

"Your best better be good enough."

Her mother hung up and didn't bother to say anything else before she did, not even goodbye. Certainly not an *I love you.*

Madison sighed and set the phone down, rubbing her temples as the headache worsened.

She could do this. She would go to the retreat, but she wouldn't do it like her mother wanted. If Aaron wanted to come, she would bring him. If not, maybe she would still go because she needed to do this one last thing. She needed to show them who she was and not back down. Because that was what this fake thing was all about. Giving her time to stand up for herself. And that's what she was going to do. To her mother's face. And if it coincided with the fact that her mom would stop her nonsense? Then that's what she would do.

She wouldn't roll over ever again.

Even if it broke her.

CHAPTER ELEVEN

"Thank you again. Seriously. I'm honestly surprised you said yes. I owe you so much."

Aaron looked over at Madison as she continued rambling her thanks. He shook his head, taking the turn up the mountain road to where the lodge was located.

"You really need to stop thanking me," he said, a smile playing on his lips. "I mean, unless you want to thank me in sexual favors. Then we can make that work."

He didn't need to look at her than to know that she was blushing all the way to the tips of her ears.

"Aaron Montgomery."

"That's my name. Pretty sure you said that last night."

She shoved at his knee lightly. He just grinned.

"You don't have to thank me for this. I get to stay at a fancy lodge, one that I've always wanted to stay at since I've heard great things about the views. And we never stay at them."

"Because Liam has his own mountain lodge," Madison said with a laugh.

"I think it's more of a cabin in the woods. A cabin-mansion, if you will. He lets some of the other cousins borrow it sometimes. And we stayed up there recently for our guys' weekend."

"I remember. I'm still kind of jealous I haven't stayed there." She winked, and Aaron smiled anew.

"I'm sure we could make that happen." He paused. "You know, for a huge family thing or something."

He said it quickly, immediately feeling awkward. He knew she felt it, too. Because going away for a weekend together, just the two of them? That wouldn't be very fake, would it? Or were they really seeing each other now?

Having a real conversation about it would've been nice, would have made things simple for them. But there was nothing simple about what they were to each other or what they were doing. Because as soon as they talked it over, they would likely walk away. He knew it. And he didn't want her to walk away from him. He didn't know what he wanted exactly, but he knew it wasn't that. So they would play things by ear and hope to hell they did it right.

Even though he knew they weren't.

"Maybe. Okay, so today is lodge day. It's going to be a lot of my father's investors, and even more people he wants to invest in him. Plus, men who just like money and pretty much roll around in it when no one's looking. Or maybe when people are looking. I don't really know the rules."

Aaron snorted and took the next turn. He wasn't a huge fan of this road. It was narrow, and they could probably fall off the cliff at any moment. He needed to pay attention to what he was doing, rather than driving them off the mountain. However, that might be preferable to what their weekend could hold.

Not that he would ever do anything to harm Madison. That was the whole point of this ruse, wasn't it?

"So, am I supposed to schmooze people or just hang out with you?" Aaron asked, keeping both hands on the steering wheel, gripping it for dear life.

"I have no idea. I'd really prefer you just standing by me the whole time so we're not alone in this. I cannot believe I said yes."

"I believe it," he grumbled.

"Because I can't stand up for myself?" she asked, her tone sounding a little hurt.

Thankful that they were on a straight part of the road, he reached over and gripped her hand, squeezing it. "That's not what I meant. I believe that you're doing this, and you told me you were doing it because you were standing up to your mother and planned to be yourself this weekend. I'm all for that. And if we get to have a couple of nice meals and maybe a little vacation in the middle of it, why not?"

"But you said you had a meeting with a big client. Now, you're missing it."

He shook his head, taking his hand back so he could pay attention to the road better.

"It was always a phone conversation. They live in New York and can't fly down all the time. They just want to talk about a few things. Not even over video. Should make it interesting for my art, right?"

"I cannot believe you can create with your hands the way you do. It's insane. I've always wanted to do something like that, but the best I can do is what I do with my cupcakes."

"First off, you know exactly what I can do with my hands," he purred.

"Aaron."

"I'm just saying. If you're going to leave a hook for a

dirty joke like that, you'll just have to deal with the ramifications."

"Just don't make those kinds of jokes in front of my parents."

"What kind of guy do you take me for?" he asked, oddly a little affronted.

"You're right. I'm just overthinking everything and am nervous."

"I'll be honest and say I'm a little nervous, too. Probably not for the same reasons you are, though."

The lodge was just around the bend, and he was grateful for that because he wanted to be able to look at her when he spoke. And that wasn't easy when he was trying not to fall off the mountain.

"Why would you be nervous? And why would it be different than my nerves?"

"First, I'm nervous that I'm going to do something that's going to make your mother hate me and ruin the whole thing we're doing here." It was bound to happen since he wasn't sure of Maeve's intentions.

"My mother will only hate you if she doesn't feel like she has a hand in orchestrating all of this."

"Uh-huh," he said, not sure what else to say because he hated that they were in this situation to begin with. He loathed how her mother treated Madison. But they were trying to change that, or at least how

Madison reacted to it. And that was the main reason he was here. Not because he wanted to be near Madison even more.

No, not that at all.

"So, is that all you're nervous about? Because that's sort of what I'm nervous about, too. Only *me* messing things up. Because I need to stand up to her, and I'm doing it. I'm not doing what she wants, other than coming to this."

"It's hard to stand up to her if you're not in front of her to do so," he said honestly. "I guess that sort of makes sense."

"Maybe a little," she said.

He smiled at her for a second before turning his attention back to the road.

She smiled over at him. "What else are you nervous about?"

"Mostly that." He wasn't sure he should say anything else, but he was already halfway there, so he might as well take the leap.

"Anything else that I need to know?"

"Not really. Just the normal guy meeting the parents thing." As if there was anything normal about what he was feeling and what they were doing.

"I see." She was silent for a moment as if going over her thoughts. "Though you have already met them."

"You're right. So, I'm not nervous at all." He let out a laugh. "Okay, fine, I'm nervous because this is for a lot longer than a dinner, but we can do this. We're *already* doing it."

Madison snorted, and he went over his words in his head.

"I meant this whole engagement thing. Though we're already doing *that,* too."

"Thanks for the laugh," she said, snorting.

"Wait, are you laughing about my performance? Because I will pull over right now and show you exactly what I mean."

He looked over as she bit her lip and he held back a groan.

"No, Aaron. No car sex while we're headed to meet my parents."

He nodded. "So, does that mean we can have car sex at other times?"

She shook her head, laughing, looking far happier than she had when they'd started the drive. He'd done that. Somehow, he'd made her feel lighter. And if he could find a way to keep doing it, he'd put everything he had into it. He was just afraid he might not be enough.

He pushed those thoughts from his mind as he pulled up to the building at the end of the winding road. "Okay, wow. This place is bigger than it looks on the internet."

Madison sighed, looking out the window. "My dad loves the lodge. Likes the fact that he sounds like a big wheeler and dealer while he's here. But it's a nice place, and the food's great. I should get over my personal feelings about it. You're going to be pampered, you're also probably going to get asked if you want to invest in something, or they're going to want to get into your inner circle to say that they know the famous Montgomerys."

"Sounds like fun," he said through gritted teeth.

"We can turn around right now if you want," she whispered.

"You know, I was thinking the same thing for you. We can go away, have a vacation of our own."

"I only got time off because I'm trying to prove to my mother that I can have happiness without her orchestrating it. And I know it seems like I'm doing the opposite with being here when she wants me to be, but she needs to see me happy, you know?"

"I do. That's why I'm here with you. So, let's do this, fiancée of mine."

She smiled.

The valet opened the door without Aaron asking, and suddenly, they were in the middle of it all. Just like they had been at her parents' house. People taking their bags, handing over a valet ticket on a very nice, crisp piece of paper, and ushering them to the front of the lodge.

Madison's mother was there, talking to a couple of women wearing pearls and nice dresses, so Aaron plastered on a smile and put his arm around Madison's waist.

She looked up at him but didn't startle.

That had to be a good sign, an indication that they were getting used to each other.

Or maybe it meant they were getting too used to each other, and it would hurt each of them even more in the end.

He should be afraid that he was getting so used to having her by his side. Because when they walked away from this, he wasn't sure how he would feel about it. Hell, he didn't know what he felt *now*. But that didn't matter at the moment because he had a part to play: the doting fiancé. He needed to get Madison through this. Because she could. He knew it, her cousin knew it, the Montgomerys knew it. Now, she just needed to realize it.

"Madison, darling," Maeve McClard said, walking forward on tall heels that made even his ankles hurt.

"Mother," Madison said, leaning forward for a kiss on the cheek.

It seemed these people were the ones that Maeve McClard wanted to impress. Therefore, she was on her best motherly behavior.

This weekend would be interesting.

"Ah. Joyce, Miranda, this is my daughter, Madison, whom I'm sure you remember. And this is her fiancé, Aaron Montgomery."

"*The* Aaron Montgomery?" either Joyce or Miranda asked.

Aaron wasn't really sure he liked how this weekend was starting out. Madison leaned into him slightly as if to give him support when it should've been the other way around. Crap.

"Yes, that Aaron Montgomery. His brother is Liam Montgomery. You know, the author? That former model who just came out to the world regarding what he's been writing under his pen name. We're so very grateful for the people in Madison's life. Oh, he also has a sister, Bristol Montgomery. You've been to her concert, I believe. We went there last year when we summered in the Hamptons. Don't you remember, darling?" Maeve asked Madison. Madison just blinked as if stunned that Maeve was namedropping as much as she was.

Hell, Aaron was a little stunned, too.

"My family is quite talented. However, I had to deal with them fighting over who got to sit in the front seat when we were younger, way before the idea of booster seats. So I don't always think of them the same as most people do."

The women tittered, though Maeve narrowed her eyes a fraction as if not happy with Aaron's humor.

Was he going to be better at it? Maybe. Would he tell the woman to go fuck herself by the end of the weekend? Most likely.

It really was going to be a long damn weekend.

"It was so nice to meet you all. Mother, we need to go check into our rooms."

"We got you one room, darling. You're engaged, after all. And we're not so old-fashioned." Her mother winked, and Aaron just blinked a couple of times, wondering where the hell this conversation was heading and exactly what he was supposed to say or do.

"Mother," Madison chided, sounding so much like Maeve it made him blink. Madison must have realized it too because she leaned back and swallowed hard. "Anyway, thanks. You know having to sneak into each other's rooms in the middle of the night probably wouldn't be too good." The other women laughed, while Maeve just narrowed her eyes more.

"Like I'd make you do the walk of shame," Aaron said, laughing and being truthful. "I'd be the one doing it, of course. But I probably shouldn't forget my key like that last time I was in my towel in the hallway. That was embarrassing."

"At least your towel didn't fall again," Madison said, grinning. He leaned down and brushed a kiss on her temple, not caring that they had an audience. However, the fact that they had an audience was exactly why he should've done it in the first place. Right?

Jesus, he wasn't doing this right. He was probably going to make mistake after mistake, but they would get through this. Because Madison was showing who she was—the humor and the fiery temptation.

He could do this.

"Go check in. Get settled. And perhaps freshen up."

"Thanks for that," Madison said dryly.

Aaron just ignored the barb. He was getting used to them. Sadly.

"Your father and I have already checked you in. He has the key. Why don't you check with him and make sure you're ready to go? He's actually off with the husbands, Joyce's and Miranda's. They're somewhere on the other side of the inn. You'll love them, Aaron.

They have a few matters they would like to talk to you about. I know that you're young now, but soon, you'll be thinking about full-time investing, and they're exactly who you need to talk with." Joyce and Miranda nodded as Maeve struck. "After all, it's time to make sure you're on the right path and up to scratch, if you're going to be marrying my baby girl." She grinned like a piranha with sharp teeth. He just rolled his shoulders back and grinned his most swoon-worthy smile. Both Joyce and Miranda seemed to notice because he saw their lips part ever so slightly.

Yeah, he knew what he was doing. And he didn't really give a flying fuck.

"Sure, sounds like an interesting weekend," he said dryly.

"We'll see if we have time for all that, Mother," Miranda said, tugging on his arm. "Thanks for checking us in and lessening our load."

"No problem, darling. Oh, I almost forgot. Guy will be here this weekend. Make sure you spend some time with him. We don't want him to feel unwanted."

Of course, Guy would be here.

It only made sense.

"I'm sure Guy can take care of himself, Mother. He's a big boy."

"You never want to be rude, darling."

"No, we wouldn't, would we, Mother?"

Aaron held back a chuckle and squeezed Madison's hip. "On that note, let's go get our key and go check out our room. This place is gorgeous. I can't wait to see the rest of it." He nodded at the others. "Ladies."

He pulled Madison away, keeping his laughter at bay.

"She is shameless," she whispered beneath her breath.

"Completely. I'm pretty sure I'm going to be a science experiment for these people."

"I'll fight them off for you."

"I thought that was my job," he whispered, liking how she wanted to defend him.

"We can do it for each other. We're in this together. Friends first, right?"

He nearly tripped over his feet. He looked down at her, swallowing hard. "Friends first, and anything else in between." He hadn't meant to say that last part, but realized it was exactly right when she smiled slightly and went up on her tiptoes to kiss his mouth. He leaned into her, not wanting to embarrass her by going any further, but needing her taste.

He was so fucking screwed.

As the night wore on, and everybody did exactly as he had assumed—wanting his money and a piece of him—he was afraid of exactly what would happen to him. To her. To them.

Because nobody really knew him or wanted to talk with him.

No, they wanted his money. They wanted his brother's money. And they wanted to get to know his family because of their name and nothing else.

They wanted a piece of him when all Aaron wanted was Madison.

That scared him more than anything. Because this was all fake. It wasn't true.

If he didn't start reminding himself of that, both he and Madison would get hurt in the end. And he was terrified that he would be the one shattered after she walked away.

He honestly didn't know who he would be once that happened.

CHAPTER TWELVE

"Seriously, you would think she would learn what kind of Botox she needs after all these years. I mean, you can't just pick the cheapest kind and expect your brows to stay in place."

Madison sipped her martini and slowly moved away from the conversation, not knowing what she was supposed to say to either help or give an opinion. She had a few friends back in college who now used Botox, and she was perfectly fine with doing whatever you wanted with your body as long as you were happy.

Maybe Madison would try it one day, though she would have to do more research into what was good and not. However, the idea that these women were complaining about someone else's Botox and putting them down wasn't something she was in the mood for.

She really wanted to be home, hanging out with her friends. Honestly, she just wanted to be with Aaron.

That should probably scare her.

It truly did because she and Aaron weren't real. And if she didn't stop to remind herself of that every ten minutes or so, she would likely end up broken.

So, all she had to do was remember that it was fake. They would walk away as friends even though they slept together and enjoyed each other's company. Somehow, they would do it. If that was even possible.

"I cannot believe she didn't get that tummy tuck," another woman sniped. Madison took another sip of her martini and moved across the room and away from her mother and her gossiping friends.

"Seriously, who does he think he is being with a woman *and* a man? I don't understand how Maeve can have that type of person in her family."

Madison nearly tripped over her feet at the conversation and turned to the three women in the corner, clearly talking about Lincoln. Lincoln, Ethan, and Holland. Three of the most generous souls Madison had ever known. Wonderful people who loved her and loved each other. Fuck these women. She was going to tell them as much.

"Excuse me?" Madison asked, her voice calm. She was on martini number two. That was probably why she was speaking up. But that's why she was here, right? To show the world and her mother that she had a spine. So, here she was, using it.

"Oh, darling. You're here. That's such a nice...dress."

Madison heard the pause in front of the word *dress*, but she didn't really care. She thought she looked great, and the little red number had made Aaron's eyes go dark when she left the room. Everyone else could go fuck themselves for all she cared.

Madison was so tired of this. Why was she here again? She wasn't supporting her father. He didn't need her here. Her mother just wanted to parade Aaron in front of her peers. Either that or somehow convince Madison to fall for Guy. But, no, she was falling for Aaron.

She blinked and pushed those thoughts from her mind. No, no, no. She could not fall for Aaron Montgomery. She could be fake with Aaron, but she could not fall for him. She needed to protect her heart somehow, even though it didn't quite feel possible.

"We were just talking about your lovely cousin. It doesn't seem that he's here."

"I'm glad," Madison said.

Lincoln and his family hadn't been invited. Maybe if he hadn't already found the loves of his life, her mother would have found a way to get him here so she could use his connections and fame. But now that he was in a triad? There was no way he would be invited to these types of things.

Madison hated that *she* was here.

Well, no more. She was done with this. She didn't want to help her parents, and she wasn't even sure she wanted them to love her anymore. They'd never love her the way she wanted anyway. She was done.

"I'm not sure he'd want to be here anyway," Madison continued. "Not with the type of people that seem to be here."

"Excuse me," one of the women said.

Joyce, that was her name. The woman who had raked her gaze all down Aaron's body when they first walked in.

No, thank you.

"I know *exactly* who's here. And Lincoln doesn't need to have any part of this. Hell, I don't think I need to. And if I hear you talking about him and his family like that again? You'll have to deal with me."

"And what exactly can you do, Madison McClard?"

"Maybe not much to a person like you. But that's the point, isn't it? I don't care what you do. But keep my cousin's family's names and their business out of your mouth."

And with that, she turned on her heel and walked away, practically shaking.

She knew her mother would hear about that later but she didn't care. She shouldn't be here. She should just go home and write this off as a loss. She didn't like the person she became when she was near these people. She was nice. She liked making people happy. That's what her coffee and cupcakes were all about. And yet, here she was, sniping at another woman for daring to say something about Lincoln. Something he would likely just ignore because he wouldn't deem them worthy of his time.

Her mother gave her a look from across the way, and she hurried off, not wanting to deal with the ramifications. Honestly, if she had to deal with her right now, she might say something she regretted later. Not that it wouldn't be true, but because she didn't want to make a scene. She didn't need to hurt her family to prove who she was. She needed them to figure it out on their own.

She made her way upstairs, sad that Aaron was off with her father, Guy, and the rest of the men. They were drinking scotch and most likely smoking, though she didn't think Aaron would since he had joked that he coughed like a teenager having his first cigarette when he had a cigar.

But he was still hanging out, pretending to be the perfect fiancé.

And she was using him.

Something she needed to change.

She walked into the suite that took her breath away every time she stepped inside. Everything was elegant and looked as if it had come from the Ritz in Paris rather than a lodge in Boulder, Colorado.

That was her family's taste—elegant and pretentious.

She wasn't going to look a gift horse in the mouth, however. She would enjoy what she had, even if she got yelled at later. And then she'd stand up for herself just like she had been doing all day.

"I'm going to take a bath," she told herself. She'd take a nice bubble bath, wait for Aaron to be finished, peel away from the others, and maybe watch a movie or have scorching hot, steamy sex.

Okay, maybe that last martini had gone straight to her head.

That was the fun part, though. She felt all warm and confident and like she could take on the world.

Maybe she could tell Aaron how she felt.

No, she couldn't. Because she didn't know.

And telling him would ruin everything.

She made her way into the bedroom part of the

suite and nearly tripped over her heels. She toed them off and looked at the very large basket sitting in the middle of the bed.

She hadn't ordered anything and wondered if she'd somehow ended up in the wrong room. She looked around, noticed her suitcase off to the side near Aaron's and frowned.

"Okay," she whispered, wondering who had sent the gift. Maybe it was from Aaron.

Giddy and a little too warm at the thought, she went to the bed and looked down at the basket, her whole body freezing.

If this was from Aaron, it would be an interesting night.

Her basket was filled to the brim with various dildos, vibrators, edible panties, condoms, lube, a couple of velvet ties, a mask, and God knew what else.

"Oh, dear God," she whispered to herself and then started to dig into the basket, wondering if this was just a practical joke. Or did Aaron have something in mind that she might be ready for?

"Is that a...? Yep, that's an anal plug," she whispered, pulling it out of the basket. Everything was new, still in its packaging, and she just blinked, wondering what the poor person who had been forced to put this in their room had thought.

Maybe Aaron had brought it up himself?

Body humming in anticipation, she finally looked at the note and went red in sheer mortification.

These are for you, have a wonderful time. Don't ask us how we knew. We saw your face. We know. Don't do anything we wouldn't do. Okay, do everything we would do. A lot. But don't tell us everything because...ew.

Madison shook with laughter, looking at the note and presents from Bristol, Arden, Holland, and Zia.

Apparently, the girls wanted her to have a very good time this weekend. And the fact that Bristol wanted nothing to do with it made total sense.

Madison's eyes widened, and she took a look at the very thick dildo in the center. She unwrapped it from its packaging, trying her best to make her middle finger and thumb reach around the girth of it.

"I don't know if that's going to fit," she mumbled to herself, holding back a laugh.

"We could always try it out."

She froze and slowly turned to look at Aaron. He stood there, his hands in his suit pants' pockets, the very visible line of his erection pushing at his zipper. He had rolled his sleeves up to his elbows, and her mouth watered.

She loved his forearms.

"Hi," she said, her voice far too breathy.

"Hi there. So, I see you packed for a good weekend," he said, his eyes dancing with laughter as well as lust and need.

"Um, this is a present. From the girls. Everything's new. And now I'm going to go hide under the bed."

"Oh no, I don't think you are." He prowled to her, fucking *prowled*. She leaned back as he tugged on her hair and crushed his mouth to hers. The thick dildo lay between them, and she squeezed it, not meaning to. He pulled back, looking down at the turgid head.

"You know, I'm pretty sure you're not going to need the dildo with me around," he promised, his eyes still shining with merriment.

"I don't know what kind of line that was, but I did not expect you to ever say something like that," she said with a laugh.

"True." He studied her face and tucked her hair behind her ear. "How drunk are you right now?"

She raised a brow.

"I tasted vodka and lemon. It mixed with my whiskey quite nicely."

"I'm not drunk at all," she said. "Completely sober after that look."

"That's good. Very good. I only had two drinks, but I'm pretty sure I can get drunk on something else right now."

"Should I ask how drunk you are?" she whispered, pressing her thighs together in anticipation.

"Not drunk at all. Now, what do you want to play with today?" he asked, his voice low. The sound went straight to her pussy.

"Um, maybe not the dildo. It honestly looks like it might hurt a bit."

He smiled and trailed his fingers up her jaw.

"What about that itty-bitty little plug I see?"

Her eyes widened, and she looked down at the basket, swallowing hard again.

"That doesn't look itty-bitty."

"Well, if you're going to want my cock in that lovely ass of yours one day, we're going to have to practice with something a little smaller."

She blinked up at him, pressing her thighs together again.

"That's something you want to do?" she asked, not knowing what she wanted his answer to be.

He reached around and slowly squeezed her ass, spreading her cheeks slightly beneath the dress.

"Anything you want to do, I'm up for. But, yeah, the idea of sliding my cock into that very sweet ass of yours? Definitely something I want to try one day. If you'll let me."

"Oh."

He kept talking about one day and in the future, and it made her just as wet as the idea of him sliding in and out of her.

Was she going to end up hurt because of it? Most likely. Did she care right now? Not in the slightest.

"Okay," she whispered.

He froze.

"Okay, what?"

"Okay, we can practice with the... You know."

He smiled.

"Nope, I don't know. You're going to have to lay it out for me."

"Aaron."

"Madison," he whined, laughing.

"Fine. I'd love if you'd put that anal plug in my ass so you can prepare me if I ever let you fuck me there. How's that?"

He threw his head back and laughed, and she pushed at his chest before he crushed his mouth to hers again. She sank into him.

"I love you talking all technical and dirty with me."

"You are going to make me pull my hair out one day."

"No, I won't. You like spending time with me. And you like my taste. And you like me touching you."

Actually, she loved it.

And she was petrified that she was falling for him. And not just his cock.

She couldn't say anything, though.

Not when it could ruin everything.

"Touch me?" she whispered.

"Let's get started."

And then he kissed her slowly, and they gently removed each other's clothes. She arched for him, needing his touch, needing everything.

She found herself on her back, his head between her legs as he licked and sucked and pleasured her.

The snap of the packaging made her swallow hard. He winked before getting up and going to set everything up.

"Keep touching your breasts and your clit, make sure you're ready for me. I'm just going to make sure everything's nice and safe for you."

She nodded, sliding her hand between her legs, her gaze on him and him alone as she thought of what he was going to do to her.

What he was already doing.

He came back, and suddenly his mouth was on her pussy again, licking and sucking. When he finished preparing her, and the plug gently probed her entrance, she stiffened for a minute. He blew on her pussy and played with her clit before meeting her gaze.

"Relax for me, take it all in."

She swallowed hard and did as he asked. When it entered her, she squirmed at the pressure, liking the way it felt but also not knowing what to feel.

Then he licked her, and he sucked. When he pressed on her clit, rubbing hard circles on the nub, she came in a burst, her entire body shaking.

He went to his knees, licked his lips, and slowly stripped himself, his gaze still stuck on her.

"Beautiful," he whispered.

"Aaron."

"Oh, we're not done yet."

He reached for something else he had prepared, and her eyes widened.

"Always wanted to try this type of vibrator," he said.

He switched it on, the buzz moving through her, her nipples hardening, and everything else going wet.

She felt as if she might come right there.

Everything was almost too much, and not just the sensations of Aaron and the toys.

When he pressed the vibrator against her clit, she shot off the bed. He laughed, a deep chuckle that went straight through her. She smiled with him before she groaned, screaming his name.

She shot off like a cannon, coming so hard she was almost embarrassed.

Honestly, there was nothing to be ashamed about when it came to Aaron. She didn't have time for that.

He always made sure she got what she wanted. What she needed. Things she hadn't even realized she desired or craved.

And when he made her come again, she felt like she was so limp she couldn't take anymore. But then Aaron was there, hovering over her.

"I'm going to fuck you with that plug in your ass. You okay with that?"

"I just need you inside me," she panted.

"Okay, then. Anything you want. I'm right here."

He slowly entered her, inch by inch, using so much care and tenderness she almost cried.

And when he licked away her tears and kissed her cheeks, she realized that she was indeed crying. She knew she should sever their connection and walk away, but she couldn't.

Not with him there. Not with so much sensation. So much...Aaron.

She moved with him, feeling full and pleasured and so loved.

The idea of the latter might just be a figment of her imagination. It could be all wrong, but she didn't care.

Instead, she arched for him. This time when she came, the tears fell harder, the sensations too much.

Everything was too much.

He came with her, filling the condom she hadn't even realized he had put on, and he called her name, whispering sweet nothings that she couldn't even comprehend.

This wasn't real. It couldn't be. They were just friends, and this was simply him taking care of her. She was here to stand up for herself, but she couldn't do it when it came to him. She was so afraid.

So, so afraid.

When he took care of her after, cleaning them both, she whimpered and snuggled into his arms, the feelings too much.

"I'm here, Madison. I'm never going away. I'm here."

She wanted the words to be real, but she couldn't believe them. Because they had started this off as a lie. How could this be reality?

How was this not a dream?

And as she fell asleep in his arms, she thought she heard words that meant something more. But they didn't.

It was just a dream. *He* was just a dream.

When they walked away from each other, it would likely kill her.

Take every ounce of the soul she had left.

So, she would forget for a moment. She would breathe.

And then she would figure out what she needed to do.

After.

CHAPTER THIRTEEN

Aaron let his head fall back as he slid his fingers into Madison's hair, groaning when she sucked his cock in deep. He opened his eyes, looked down to see her blond and pink hair bobbing over his dick, her mouth a warm, wet heat that made him want to come right then and there. But he held back, not wanting this to end.

He had woken up with a hard-on from hell, needing to come, but had held back and slowly placed himself between her thighs. He woke her with an orgasm, eating her out until both of them were sweaty and needy. Instead of plunging inside her like he wanted to and fucking them both into the best morning ever, he rolled onto his back at her urging. He was now living his best life with her on his dick, sucking him as if she'd waited forever to do so.

He couldn't breathe, couldn't focus. All he wanted to do was stay in bed with Madison for the rest of the day, even though he knew he couldn't.

This was bliss.

Pure fucking bliss.

They had things to do today, an agenda thanks to the retreat and everything that had to do with why they had come to the lodge in the first place. But all of that was pushed from his mind because all he wanted was to be in the woman on top of him. To see how long they could go making each other come, perhaps until the sun went down.

Madison hummed on his dick, hollowing her cheeks to squeeze him even tighter.

He groaned, lifted his hips without conscious thought, and then tried to lower them, attempted to give her control. She dug her hand into his thigh, groaned, clearly needing more.

She licked and sucked, and when she cupped his balls, he was a goner. He tugged on her hair to pull her away.

She lifted her head and licked her lips. At that look, the look of a pleased and sated woman, he came, putting his hand over the tip of his dick so he came there instead of on her tits like he sort of wanted to. He hadn't asked permission, and he wasn't about to come down her throat or anywhere else without asking.

Madison licked her lips again and grinned at him. He reached around with his clean hand to slide his fingers along her hip, up her rib cage, and to the gentle slope of her breast.

"Good morning," he said, his voice a little rough.

"Good morning. I guess that's one way to wake up."

He laughed, shook his head, and pulled her down to kiss her.

"I guess so. I think we're late."

She pulled away and looked at the clock on the bedside table.

She cursed. "My mother is going to kill us."

"Maybe. Or she won't notice because she'll be too busy with everybody else, and we can just slink in the back."

"We have twenty minutes to get downstairs for breakfast, and I have sex hair."

He grinned and tugged on her hair a bit.

"Hell yeah, you do. Nice and beautiful, well-fucked hair."

"That sounds like you fucked my hair rather than me all night."

Aaron cringed.

"Fine. I'm not good with the whole words thing in the morning without my coffee. Although, you waking me up like that is pretty much the best way."

"I do believe that you were the one who woke me up with your head between my thighs."

"That is true. I'll have to do it again."

He ignored the annoying clutch in his heart at the thought. Would this charade of theirs be over once they left the lodge? She was already standing up for herself to the point where he knew she saw what he did: a strong, confident woman who didn't need to deal with her family.

He didn't know what they were doing now. Were they just playing a game with each other or ignoring the fact that they had no idea what was up?

He pushed the thoughts from his mind because he'd had an amazing morning so far, and he didn't want to ruin it with reality.

They rolled out of bed and took a shower together, being quick about it. Not because he didn't want to fuck her right there or touch her or taste her or do other things to linger, but because they really were running late.

He went about pulling out her clothes for her, mostly because she had mentioned what she was going to wear as she blew her hair dry. He walked around the suite in nothing but a towel, getting everything ready for their day. He hoped he was doing it right. If not, she could fix it, but he didn't want her mother to be any more annoyed than she already was just by Madison breathing.

He snorted at that idea and made his way back to the mirror next to Madison to start his routine.

Her hair was dry, put up in some kind of knot at the back of her head with tendrils flowing all around her face.

"Hey, I like the hair."

She snorted.

"It's not completely dry and has a bit of a wave to it, but this way I can hide some of the pink."

"I hate that you have to hide it at all."

"Me, too. I normally wouldn't care, but this makes things easier. Not necessarily for my mother but for the others. I'm not a huge fan of being the center of attention."

"You still look great, so what do I know?" He reached around and smacked her ass over her panties, and she narrowed her eyes at him.

"Don't you get all frisky with me. We are running really late."

He leaned down and kissed her hard on the mouth.

"We're still getting used to this whole getting ready next to each other thing. It's kind of hard when you distract me."

"You know I've never actually gotten ready next to a man before. I don't like that you're nearly done, and I still have to put on my makeup and pick out my clothes."

"I took out what you said you were going to wear last night. Is that okay?" he asked, leaning forward to check his face for toothpaste marks or anything.

"Oh, great. That's great." She blushed, and he frowned.

"Did I do something wrong? You had the blow dryer going, or I would have told you what I was doing."

"No, you did everything right. I'm just not used to this whole coupling thing. Even though I don't think we're a couple. Right? No, don't answer that. Please don't."

She rushed off to the bedroom, and Aaron stood there, blinking as he stared into the mirror.

"Fuck," he whispered under his breath.

They were not ready for that conversation, especially because he knew what the answer would be. He would walk away from her, and then he wouldn't know what to do.

Because everything was fake. This was all a façade.

An idea where they could pretend in order for her to find herself. And she was doing it. She was beautiful and brilliant, but she wasn't for him.

Even though he thought he might already be in love with her.

"Fuck," he whispered again and then shook his head, washed his face, and got ready for the day.

As soon as they were ready to go, her in a light dress, and him in khaki pants and a white button-down shirt with his sleeves rolled up, she slid on her heels, went to her tiptoes, and kissed him softly on the mouth. "I'm sorry."

He frowned. "Why?" he asked.

"I'm grateful that you're doing all of this for me. But I'm not treating you right. I'm doing this wrong. So, after this weekend, we'll talk. But for now? Let's just do what we've been doing and have fun."

He swallowed hard and nodded. "I can do that. And, Madison? You're not taking advantage of me. This place has great food, great views, and I'm getting some inspiration for my work. Plus, I like hanging out with you. We're friends. Always."

She smiled up at him then, and he hoped like hell he wasn't lying to himself about that. Because he loved her.

And he was so screwed.

They went downstairs to the dining area, their hands linked as they made their way in, nodding at others as they did.

Though they were around twenty minutes late, people were just now sitting down for breakfast, and Aaron was grateful.

"It seems like everybody had a bit of a lay-in," she whispered.

"Thank God."

"You're right. I wouldn't want to deal with the fact that we're late and my hair being only somewhat done."

"You still look hot."

"Thanks. Honestly, I don't care. I would have just let the pink show, but that would require straightening my hair, and I just don't have the energy today. Somebody wore me out."

Aaron practically preened on his way to an empty table. As soon as they stood near, Mark gestured him over to his table.

"Madison, come sit with your mother and me."

"Yay," Madison whispered under her breath, and Aaron did his best not to laugh out loud at that.

"Hi, Daddy," Madison whispered before kissing her father on the cheek. "Good morning."

"Good morning, you two. Glad you decided to show up."

Her dad gave Aaron a look with a raised brow, and Aaron did his best not to play with this collar, knowing the man likely knew exactly what had happened the night before.

Jesus Christ, he hoped he didn't know exactly. That was not something Aaron ever needed to discuss with anyone but Madison.

Because the kinky shit they'd gotten up to last night? The best night of his life. Ever.

And now he had a feeling her father knew everything and would judge him. And probably kill and bury him in the woods out behind the lodge.

It could happen.

He'd read books about it.

But given everything he had done to Madison the night before?

Oh, yeah, Aaron probably deserved it. And more.

"Everybody seems to be taking their time this morning," Mark said, looking down at his phone. "Which is fine with me. I hate early mornings."

Aaron pulled Madison's chair back, letting her sit down before sitting on the other side of her.

She snorted at her father's words.

"You have worked early every morning for as long

as I've known you. I don't actually believe you when you say that you hate early mornings."

Mark gave her a look that would have sent most people into hysterics, but she just stood her ground.

That was his Madison. Stronger than she knew.

No, not his, he reminded himself. Never his.

"I went to work early so I could come home to you and your mother in the evenings. Just because I did it, didn't mean I liked it."

He seemed uncomfortable at his pronouncement before he went back to looking at his phone. Madison pointed at him a couple of times, confusion on her face.

He didn't blame her. That was almost a declaration of love from the man who Aaron wasn't sure had ever said those words.

Or maybe he looked too deeply into it.

That's what he was good at.

"Where's Mother?" Madison asked as the waiter came around with coffee.

Aaron added cream to his, then took a big gulp, needing the caffeine after the night they'd had. They hadn't gotten much sleep, and when Madison took a big gulp of hers as well, he knew she was feeling it, too. Hopefully, her father wouldn't notice.

"She'll be over soon. She needed to talk with Joyce about one of the committees that she's running." He sounded dismissive of what Maeve McClard did, but maybe Aaron was wrong. After all, he didn't like the man. Tolerated his wife even less. But that didn't mean he understood them. And he didn't like the way they treated Madison. Or even him, for that matter.

"Okay, do you know what's on the agenda for today?"

"Not a clue. I have meetings with a few of my clients for most of the day, but I know your mother has something planned. She'll let you know what you need to do."

"And I'll let her know if I'm able."

"Whatever. Just don't make your mother angry. I'm not in the mood for that."

He went back to his phone, texting as quickly as a teenager did, and Aaron gave Madison a look.

She didn't say anything, simply shook her head. When Maeve finally came to the table, she wasn't alone.

No, Guy was there.

A smug smile on his face.

Aaron really hated the guy.

"Good morning, darling," Maeve said, reaching around to air-kiss Madison's cheek. "I spotted Guy about to sit alone. We just can't have that. He'll join us for breakfast."

Guy moved her chair back, and Maeve took a seat. Mark narrowed his eyes at the movement before going back to his phone.

"Good morning, Guy. Mother. I hope you had a pleasant evening." Aaron wanted to growl at how agreeable Madison sounded, but he knew she was trying. Just like he was.

"I'm sure you had an eventful one," Maeve said, practically snapping. While Aaron wanted to think that maybe she was discussing what Madison and he had gotten up to the night before, he had a feeling it had more to do with what had happened between Joyce and Madison.

He was grateful that he hadn't been there. If he had, he probably wouldn't have been as nice as Madison, and she had been anything but nice for once.

He could not believe the nerve of some people, but he couldn't change their opinions either.

Madison had stood up for her family, though, so fuck everyone else. That was a refrain he said often lately, but he couldn't help it. He was so tired of human beings.

"Anyway, I fixed what happened with Joyce last night. She just assumed you had too much alcohol. You know how it is."

"That's not what happened, Mother."

"It's fine, you know Joyce. She's the one who drank too much."

Maeve rolled her eyes, and Aaron held back a frown, wondering what Maeve had meant by that. Was she standing up for Madison? Or was she just playing games? He did not understand this woman, and she made him more confused than ever.

"Oh good, the waiter is here. I could use some coffee."

They ordered their drinks, and everyone refilled their mugs, with Maeve getting her first cup.

Aaron was tired, probably a little *too* tired for dealing with Maeve and her games. But Madison needed him, and the way she leaned into him and laughed and looked at him like he was her whole world made him feel like this was real. That it wasn't fake.

She would never play games with him like that, and he believed it.

It was hard to want more when he didn't know what they had to begin with.

Or maybe he was overthinking.

They spoke about nothing important, mostly Mark's job, and Guy's investments. Aaron nodded along, mainly paying attention to Madison and no one else.

When she did the same with him, he felt like he was on top of the world.

However, he was afraid of what would happen when the world came crashing down, gravity pulling them to their deaths.

"Madison, Guy was just telling us about a little coffee shop that reminded him of yours. You should go with him to look at it."

Aaron blinked, pulling himself out of his thoughts as Madison froze next to him.

"Oh, it's like mine?"

"Yes," Guy said, his voice smooth and cultured.

"You mentioned wanting to start a franchise. This might be a good way to begin that. At least, get the lay of the land. What do you think, darling?" Maeve prompted.

Aaron had no idea what this woman was playing at. Why did it sound as if she suddenly cared about Madison's job? Was she turning over a new leaf? Not likely. No, this was more about wanting to get Guy alone with Madison. It was all a manipulation.

But Aaron saw the curiosity in Madison's gaze, and he knew it wasn't about the man. It couldn't be. Guy was a nice dude, he made her laugh, just like Aaron did, but she didn't want him. Right? No, that was just some odd jealousy that had nothing to do with them talking.

She wanted to know about the coffee shop. That was it. Right?

"That sounds wonderful," Madison said, looking at Aaron. "What do you say? Do you want to go?"

Aaron cringed.

"I'd love to. You know I love your cupcakes and coffee." He grinned, leaning down and almost brushing a kiss along her lips before he remembered where they were. Instead, he tucked her hair behind her ear. "But..."

She smiled up at him, her eyes bright. "What's wrong?"

"I have that meeting with my client. I can't get out of it."

"We'll wait, then."

"No, no," Maeve said. "You shouldn't have to wait. It's the perfect day for visiting and seeing the shop. You can take Aaron down another time. I'm sure he's seen your store enough. Right, Mr. Montgomery?"

Mr. Montgomery?

What was this woman playing at?

He could not get a read on her, but he wasn't sure he really wanted to.

"You should go," Aaron said, clearing his throat. He reached out and kissed Madison's hand. "You have been talking about wanting to expand for a while.

Seeing a coffee shop in a place like this could be perfect for you."

"I'd rather see it with you," she whispered.

He was aware that the others were listening, but he didn't know what to say.

So what if they heard? This was what this whole game was about, wasn't it?

He just hated that he even thought it was a game.

What was he doing?

Why was he letting himself fall like this?

He shouldn't.

This would only hurt them both in the end.

"You should go," he said again. "Have fun. And tell me all about it. And then we can go again later."

She smiled and nodded, searching his face before turning back to Guy. "I would love to go see it."

Guy grinned, looking smug as fuck. But then again, so did Maeve.

Aaron had a horrible feeling that he had just played into whatever the woman wanted.

But did it matter?

She was seemingly taking an interest in Madison's life, and even if that wasn't the case, Madison was standing up for herself. All was going according to plan.

Aaron had taken the heat off her.

And when she walked away, he'd have to figure out

exactly what to do about the feelings wrapping themselves around his heart. Feelings that wouldn't go away, even if he told himself repeatedly that they meant nothing.

That this was all pretend.

Because, deep down, he knew there was nothing fake about what he felt for Madison.

He was so fucked.

CHAPTER FOURTEEN

Madison was confused. Why had Aaron seemed so odd at breakfast? Perhaps it was the same reason *she* felt weird.

She was falling for him. He was only supposed to be her friend. The one she could rely on as they traversed these odd circumstances they were in, but she was falling for him. And she shouldn't.

He would walk away when the time came, and she would have to let him. He was doing this because he was a good guy, because he believed in helping others, and she couldn't stand in his way and force him to love her. She wouldn't let herself acknowledge what she felt for him more than she already had. Once she did that, she would shatter into a thousand pieces, all because she couldn't focus.

"What's with that sad look on your face?" Guy asked from her side, looking suave and debonair.

She looked up at that strong jaw, those piercing gray eyes, and the slight stubble he had on his face that made him look even sexier.

She didn't know why he had allowed himself to be caught in her mother's web. She would always be wary of him, but he seemed nice. Perhaps she would have been attracted to him under other circumstances, and may have agreed to being set up with him. But not now. Especially not when her heart belonged to Aaron.

"I'm just thinking. Long morning."

Not quite a lie, not quite the truth.

"I'm sure Aaron is glad he has time to focus on his clients. After all, he does need to work and not spend all his time with you."

She frowned at Guy's tone and looked up at him.

"I never once thought that he needed to spend all his time with me." She just wanted him to because she liked being near him and enjoyed the sound of his voice and the way he made her feel.

Even if she couldn't quite put her finger on exactly what that was. An unnamed emotion crawled through her that said she wanted him to stay by her side forever.

Was that love? Obsession? Or denial of the fact that he would never be hers?

"Madison? Is everything okay?"

She shook herself out of her reverie and looked up at Guy. "Sorry, let's go see this coffee place. What's it called again?"

"Boulder Cup."

"Boulder Cup?" she asked, frowning. "Really?"

"The coffee and the pastries are much better than the name."

"It's so hard coming up with coffee shop names these days. All the good ones are taken."

"I don't know, yours sounds like a delight."

He purred the words, and she nearly blushed, but it wasn't Aaron saying them, so she simply shrugged.

"My friends always said my cupcakes were sinful, so it turned into that."

"You know, I've never actually tasted your...cupcakes."

He paused before the last word, and she barely resisted the urge to roll her eyes.

Obvious, much?

She was engaged. It might not be genuine, but Guy didn't know that. She didn't like that he was being so forward and acting as if she weren't taken. Like he could just flirt with her however he wanted.

She made sure there was space between them even though he constantly moved closer to her.

She would get through this quickly, see how the Boulder Cup was set up, and figure out if she really wanted to franchise her business. She didn't think she would end up in a place like this, most likely in another college town like Fort Collins. But if she did decide to expand into a little more boutique-like place up in the mountains, maybe this would be a good start.

Either way, she loved going into different coffee shops. Only, she wished she was here with Aaron rather than with Guy.

She knew Aaron needed to work, and the fact that he had even come to the retreat at all was wonderful. He hadn't been forced into coming to the lodge with her, but she sure felt that way.

He had a job to do, and it wasn't like he could bring his furnace and his blowpipe with him everywhere. Yes, she knew he sketched out many of his pieces before-hand, but that wasn't what he was doing now. No, he was talking with a client on the phone from a hotel, all because she needed him, and he had come for her.

Yes, she was in love with Aaron Montgomery. And she had no idea what to do about it.

"Here we are," Guy said after a moment. She looked around at the tiny little mountain town they were in, everything looking picturesque.

It was very touristy, but it worked. The outsides

of the buildings all looked very similar, but she figured they would each be a little different once you got inside. When you were in mountain towns like this, even a McDonald's had to have a particular architecture and aesthetic that fit the ambiance of the area rather than a typical fast food place.

They went inside the Boulder Cup, and she looked around at the wood carvings on the walls, the gorgeous stained wood rafters, and wondered if she could add something like that to her place. Maybe not until she had the second location in mind and more than a few written down notes and hours of research.

She'd have to talk with her cousin and Aaron about it and get their thoughts.

The idea that she wanted to talk about it with Aaron should surprise her, but not really. He was easy to talk to, except for when it came to discussing her feelings. But everything else? It was like he understood her completely.

"So, what will you have?"

Madison looked at the perfectly hand-drawn menu and smiled.

"Let me see. A latte of some sort, but they have so many delicious flavors. Maybe a toasted marshmallow?"

It was the middle of summer, but still, that sounded great.

"They have it iced if it's too hot for you."

Guy said that as if it were an innuendo, and she was confused. Still, she let him do what he needed. She didn't understand what he wanted from her, but she wasn't going to give it to him, regardless.

He ordered for her. She wasn't too happy about that, but she allowed it, and would have said something if he'd forced her to get it iced. When he paid, she let him because he would likely make a scene if she protested.

She was going to be nice. Not because her mother wanted it, but because she was just decent. Guy seemed to be a good person, who was merely humoring her mother, but Madison still didn't understand what he got out of this whole thing. He didn't want her. Maybe as a prize, but not in the way she wanted to be needed.

Not in the way she wanted Aaron. Or the way she wished he desired her.

She quickly pushed that thought from her mind, knowing that she couldn't let herself go down that road. It wouldn't be fair to either of them if she allowed herself to keep thinking that this could be something more than what it was.

She and Guy took a table outside on the deck, the mountains surrounding them, the air clean and fresh.

"I love it out here. They have a great location."

"They do, and they're thinking about selling."

She froze, looking over at him. "Really?"

"Really. It's owned by an older couple that wants to retire soon, and their children don't want any part of the family business. This place has had a lot of reincarnations over time, but the same owner no matter what."

"How do you know all this?"

"I have my ways," he said with a smile that worried her.

She didn't like that expression.

And she didn't know why.

"I'm not anywhere near ready to buy a place like this. And I don't even know if I want to come up here or start in Fort Collins like I was planning."

"Why would you want to go to a dirty college town when you could have a place like this?"

She narrowed her eyes. "Fort Collins is beautiful. Every place in Colorado is. And I'd probably do better business up there anyway."

"If you want to deal with the college clientele and that riffraff."

"I think we have very different ideas of what *riffraff* is," she said through gritted teeth.

"Perhaps."

She sipped her coffee, the perfect temperature for her tongue, and her mood. It was sweet, the coffee strong and perfectly brewed. She was a little jealous that she didn't have this in her shop and might have to make a version of it, one that wasn't stealing but reminded her of how good this was.

She took a few more sips, tasting the subtle notes, and thought of a cupcake to match.

A s'mores cupcake? With a toasted marshmallow on top? Or maybe marshmallow inside? A fluff of some sort?

"What are you thinking about that's making you look so beautiful?" Guy asked, and she looked up, snorting.

"Really? That's what you're going with?"

"What?"

"Never mind. But you don't need to keep doing this, Guy. I'm engaged. Nothing you say will change that."

He snorted. "We both know that's not real."

She blinked, looking up at him, all thoughts of marshmallow leaving her mind. "Excuse me?"

"A secret fiancé just when your mother finally finds you a partner? No, your mother and I know it's fake. I can understand you being scared about marrying a man you don't know. But I am the perfect guy for you. No pun intended. Your mother assured me that the more I got to know you, the more I'd know it's the truth."

Madison was grateful that she had gotten her coffee to go in a recyclable cup. She stood. "Well, thank you for that."

He frowned. "For what?"

"Thank you for showing me this place, but mostly, for making sure I knew I was making the right decision."

"Excuse me?"

"I'm not for you. We both know that. I don't know what your end game is, but I don't want this place, and I don't want you."

"You don't know what you're missing."

"I can clearly see what I'd be missing. And it's not much. Go back to my mother and tell her that you failed. I want nothing to do with you. I'll do the same. And you can't change my mind."

"You're not truly engaged. I don't know why you keep pretending that you are."

"And I don't know why you keep harping on this."

She turned on her heel and began the long walk back, not knowing what she was going to say to her mother. She was so pissed off. She hated that Guy was just another person who wanted to control her.

She had Lincoln and his new family. They weren't the ones who had raised her, but they were the only real family she had. She had known this for far too long, though chose to ignore it. Instead, what had she done? She had done whatever she could to get her family to love her.

To *like* her.

And she was hurting herself and others trying to make that happen when it never would.

She turned the corner when someone grabbed her elbow, knocking the coffee out of her hand. It splashed on the cement around her, the cup rolling into the street. Hot coffee splashed over her legs, and she let out a startled scream, taking a few steps back. Or at least she tried to, but Guy had his hand around her elbow, tugging her close.

"Let go of me."

"Fuck you. How dare you?"

"How dare I?" she asked, shaking.

"How dare you talk to me like that? Your mother arranged this. And it's what's best for you. If you didn't have your head in your ass and in the clouds, maybe you'd realize what this would do for you. You're not going to change what I've been promised."

Fear crawled up her spine. She tugged against his grip, but he kept holding onto her. She knew she'd probably have bruises later.

"Let me go," she said, wishing someone was around, but they were around the corner just enough that there wasn't anybody to hear her scream.

"Fine. I'm going to get you in the end. I always get what I want. Always." And then he let her go, and she stumbled back, tripping over the lid of her coffee. She nearly fell but righted herself, then turned, only to find the place where he had been now empty.

Guy had left her, and she wasn't sure where he'd gone.

She needed to get back to the lodge.

She needed to see Aaron.

She'd had no idea what Guy hid beneath the surface, and now that she'd seen it, she wanted nothing to do with it.

She just wanted to see Aaron.

She wanted this to be over.

She froze. No, not completely over.

Because as soon as she got back home, everything *would* be finished.

She was done playing a game. She was done lying so she didn't have to face the consequences.

Only now, she would have to face the real ones.

Aaron would walk away as soon as this was over, and she would be left alone.

She practically ran towards the lodge, hoping to hell that Guy didn't find her along the way.

He had just gotten angry. He wouldn't really hurt her, would he?

The fact that she didn't know the answer to that worried her, but she would get to Aaron no matter what. She made her way as quickly as possible towards the lodge. Aaron would help her. Or at least he would help her help herself.

And then she'd figure out what to do after she held him.

CHAPTER FIFTEEN

aron was in a fucking bad mood, and he had no idea how to make it better. Madison was off with Guy, the two of them probably having coffee and getting to know one another.

Guy didn't seem all that bad, even though he was seemingly going along with Maeve's plans. But he didn't seem like too much an asshole from what Aaron could tell, at least from the little he knew about the other man. Maybe he would be a good person for Madison. For all Aaron knew, the two had more in common than Madison and he did. It wasn't like Madison and Guy dating would ruin Aaron's friendship with Madison like he feared would happen if he and Madison weren't careful. She was practically family, and here he was, tainting what they had because he just couldn't hold back.

He was such a fucking asshole. He needed to keep from hurting her. Maybe Guy was the answer.

He grumbled, finished his single beer for the day, and sank back into the couch cushions in their suite.

He had been in a few beautiful suites and hotel rooms over time thanks to his career and the fact that his brother spoiled him, but he'd never been in a place this nice. They had a fricking living room in this thing, with a couch big enough to fit him. He was a large man, over six feet and wide with muscle. He needed the strength for his job, and he always tried his best to bulk up like his brothers did.

So the fact that this couch was comfortable *and* could fit his entire body? That meant it was a big fucking sofa. Though it didn't overwhelm the room. The suite had to be one of the largest and nicest he'd ever been in.

And he had no idea what he was doing here.

Things were getting so complicated with Madison. He should have known they would get that way. He'd announced their engagement before he even spoke to her. What had he been thinking? Daisies and happiness and things going right the first time out of the gate? Not so much.

He and Madison needed to talk. He knew that. Because as soon as they walked away from this lodge, the charade would be over. It had to be. She wasn't the same person she had been even a couple of days before. Or maybe the reality was that she was the same person she had been all along, but now wasn't hiding behind layers.

He didn't know where he fit in with any of her future plans. And the fact that he didn't, worried him.

He hated that, but he wasn't sure how to fix it. Not yet. Not unless the two of them actually spoke, something that needed to happen soon.

The door opened, and he pulled himself from his thoughts into the present as he looked up at Madison, now standing in the doorway, her eyes wide. He didn't know what that look was about, but relief flooded her face as soon as she saw him, and then she rushed over to hug him hard.

"Hey there," he said, confused. He kissed the top of her head.

"Hey."

"How was coffee?" he asked, gruff an a little annoyed for some reason. He didn't like the fact that she had spent the afternoon with Guy. He felt like he could practically smell him on her, even though he couldn't, and it bothered him.

Why was he having thoughts like such a jealous asshole?

Were they together in truth? He didn't know. Because why would they fucking talk about anything and make things easy?

She ran her hands down his back and sighed.

He didn't like that sound. Had she had fun, then?

"Coffee was okay.

"Okay," he said, knowing he sounded petulant.

"Yes, I had a marshmallow thingy."

"Marshmallows are good." See? Not a child. He could have an actual conversation and not growl. Was he growling? Oh yeah, he kind of was.

"I'm thinking about adding marshmallow cupcakes of some sort to the menu at Sin. Maybe a s'mores."

His stomach rumbled at that, and she laughed.

"Apparently, I'm craving marshmallows."

"All that ooey-gooey goodness in the center?" she asked.

"Should I say creamy goodness?" he asked, his cock hardening in his pants, pressing against her belly.

Her eyes widened. He leaned down, tugging her hair a bit. When her lips parted, her eyes going dark, he crushed his mouth to hers, needing her.

"You might have been out with him today, but you're here with me right now."

She pulled away, confusion in her gaze.

"It wasn't a date. Far from it."

"Fine." He kissed her again, knowing he was an asshole, but he wanted her taste. She kissed him right back, tugging on his shirt. He pulled away, letting her undo the buttons then dropping it to the floor. He slid his hands up her thighs and tugged her dress over her head in one quick movement.

She gasped, and he glanced down at her tiny little panties and the lacy bra that allowed him to feel her nipples beneath the cups.

"You wore this while you were out with him? Did he know what you were wearing under your dress?" he asked, his voice a growl. He pinched her nipple through the lace, and she gasped, sighing as she toed off her shoes, the action making her body rub against his too-hard dick.

"Only for you. Promise."

"We'll see about that."

He reached around to her ass and squeezed before slapping her rounded flesh, hard.

She gasped again, and he grinned at her.

"Did you like that?"

"As long as you're not punishing me. Because there's no way I'm going to let you do that."

She gave him a weird look, and he frowned before

kissing her again, rubbing his hand over the spot he had spanked. "Never punishment. Only pleasure. Promise."

He knew the two of them liked rough sex, just as they liked soft sex. But he was never going to hurt her. Fuck, no matter what, he would never hurt her. Even if it meant walking away completely when things dissolved between them.

But for now, all he wanted was her. Her taste. He craved it.

"Now, what were we talking about? Warm ooey-gooey goodness?" he asked, reaching around to slowly slide his fingers over her slit.

"I don't know if I'm going to be able to make those marshmallow cupcakes if you keep talking like that."

"I think you should. Every time I lick one up, I'll meet your gaze, and you'll know what I'm thinking about."

"See? I'm not sure I'm going to be able to make those cupcakes."

"Well, then, I'll just have to ensure that you do." He paused, not knowing why he was saying the words he was. "Unless you'd rather eat them with Guy."

She froze and then pushed at him. "What the hell?"

"I'm just saying. You two seemed to hit it off."

Why was he saying this? He was acting like a jealous bastard.

"No. I'm with you, you asshole. At least while we're figuring this out. Stop it. You have me practically naked, your hand's on my pussy, and you're talking about another guy? What the hell is wrong with you?"

"Nothing's wrong with me. I'm just saying shit that I shouldn't. I'm so sorry." He kissed her again, and she folded her arms under her generous breasts before finally sinking into him.

"I don't want to talk about Guy. It's just you and me. Like you promised. Okay? We'll figure everything out later."

He didn't know what they would figure out, but he obeyed, leaning in to kiss her again, this time softly. His hands slid down her body to squeeze her hips.

"I really am sorry."

"Me, too. Now kiss me again. I liked the growly stuff. I don't like it when we're fighting."

"I thought fighting could lead to the growly stuff," he teased.

"Let's just have makeup sex and call it a day. I could really use you."

"You're just using me?"

"That's not what I meant," she said quickly, her face blushing.

"I know, baby. I know." He kissed her again, this time lifting her off her feet as he led her through the living room area to the suite's bedroom. She wrapped her legs around his waist, kissing him softly as he petted her before gently laying her on the bed.

He went to his knees, pulling her so her ass was at the edge of the bed, and blew on her pussy over her lace thong.

"So pretty and wet," he whispered.

"Aaron. Stop staring. It's embarrassing."

He pinched her thigh, and she squeaked. "There's nothing to be embarrassed about. I love every inch of you."

She froze, and he knew he had blundered. He hadn't meant to say the word *love*, even in a casual context. Neither of them was ready for that. And he knew she might never be. He was only a distraction, merely a placeholder until she got ready for the next phase of her life.

"You're so fucking sexy," he growled, trying to make it seem like he was just talking about her body and nothing else.

She relaxed, and he swallowed hard, wondering why that hurt. Did she not want to know how he felt?

Of course, not. Honestly, he didn't know for sure either.

He pulled her panties to the side, revealing her before leaning down and sucking on her clit. Her hips shot off the bed, so he pushed her back down, needing her taste.

Craving her.

He groaned and played with her slit before licking some more.

"You taste so sweet. Just like a cupcake."

"Aaron," she chided. He chuckled roughly against her pussy, knowing that his beard scraped her, the sensation probably sending vibrations all the way up to her nipples. She had told him that once, so he kept doing it, knowing she loved it.

He was learning what she liked, what she loved, what things she wanted more of.

He was starting to need her in every way possible. And that worried him. So fucking much. But there was no going back now, at least not for him.

He sucked again, laving and swiping long licks up her pussy. When she came, she practically shook off the bed. He grinned and pulled back slightly.

Standing and palming his dick over his pants, he went to the suitcase near the bed and pulled out a few more toys.

Her breaths came in pants as she cupped her breasts over her bra and licked her lips.

"Are you ready?" he asked, holding up the plug.

"Only for you."

He didn't want to think that was true because it'd be too hard to walk away. So, he leaned down and kissed her, taking her breath away before slowly working the plug into her, inserting it gently so as not to hurt her. He never wanted to hurt her. That was the one vow he could promise her and keep.

When she arched for him, he grinned and kissed her again before reaching around to help her undo her bra.

Her breasts fell free, and he sucked on them, pinching the nipples hard until they were delicate little peaks that went from peach to cherry red.

So fucking sexy," he growled against her breasts.

"I need you. Let me see." She reached out to him, squeezing his dick through his pants. He groaned, pulling away.

"Aaron," she whined.

"Need to get a condom first." He swallowed hard, stripped down so he was naked, his dick slapping against his belly. Her eyes went wide, turning dark with need.

She looked so fucking sexy there. It was hard for him to breathe.

He slid the condom over his dick, knowing that her gaze followed every movement.

And then he went back to the edge of the bed, tugged on her hips so she scooted towards him, and then flipped her onto her stomach.

"Aaron," she gasped.

"On your hands and knees, baby. I can't wait to watch this little plug of yours dance as I fuck you hard."

The plug had a pink diamond on the end that shined as he looked down and spread her cheeks.

"So fucking gorgeous, all decorated for me. Are you ready?"

"Past ready. Now fuck me already," Madison ordered. He grinned, squeezing her hip again before slamming hard into her.

They both groaned. The sensation of his cock filling her, stretching her to her limits, made them both shake. He leaned over her, licking up her spine before biting gently on her shoulder. She moaned, arching into him, wiggling her ass. He grinned before pulling out and slamming home again.

"Aaron!"

She kept pushing back, so he pushed forward, fucking her hard—harder than ever. He knew he would probably leave bruises, but she kept pushing, begging for him to keep going. So, he did. He might leave marks, but he would never hurt her. She would get what she wanted, nothing less, and nothing more.

He couldn't see her face in this position, couldn't see what secrets her eyes held. Would he see love? Would it just be lust?

He didn't know if he wanted to see, so he kept her on all fours, tugging on her hair but not seeing her face.

Or maybe he remained this way because he didn't want her to see *his* face. There would be no hiding what he felt. Not right now. And it scared him.

Finally, she shattered, coming with his name on her lips. He followed right after, shaking. Needing to breathe.

He nearly fell on top of her. It took him a moment to stop shaking so he could move so they were lying with her back to his front. He was still deep inside her, holding her close.

He let out a sigh and ran his hands up and down her sweat-slick hips then sighed before cupping her breasts, needing to touch her.

"I still feel so full," she whispered, her voice soft and dreamy.

He nibbled her neck before kissing her again.

He loved the way she angled her head so he could reach her lips when he stretched.

"I love that you like it," he whispered.

"I wasn't expecting to come up here and do this. But I still love it."

Good," he whispered. Are you going to kiss me again?" she whispered. He nodded before sliding out of her and then groaned.

Her whole body shook, and he took care of the condom before coming back and holding her close.

He kissed her, gently petting her. He still craved her, needed more.

"Wow," he whispered.

"Wow."

She looked into his eyes, and he wanted to say something, though he wasn't sure that he could.

"Let's just take it slow, then?"

"Slow," she whispered, and his heart clenched.

"We'll figure this out. You and me, right?"

"Okay. That works." He kissed her again. They made love one more time, his cock impossibly hard despite it being so soon after their first session. They went slow this time, the touch achingly sweet. He groaned, knowing that he loved her.

And he had no idea what he was going to do when he had to walk away.

CHAPTER SIXTEEN

The next morning, thighs aching, Madison towel-dried her hair and just shook her head at Aaron as he raked his gaze over her.

"Really? We just had sex in the shower. A lot of sex in the shower. I think I'm going to end up walking bowlegged for the rest of the day at this point."

"Hey, your mother did mention that she wanted to try horseback riding today if the weather held up."

Madison rolled her eyes. "No, do not mention my mother when we're talking about sex."

His whole body shuddered, and she laughed, knowing he deserved it.

"I cannot believe you brought that up."

"You're the one who mentioned my mother. I'm just saying."

"Fine. I will refrain from touching you. That way, you can stop walking so gingerly."

He reached out and tugged on her towel a bit. She was grateful that she had tucked the ends in at the tops of her breasts tightly enough that it didn't fall to the floor so easily.

"Aaron."

"What? I'm not allowed to look?"

"If you look, I'm going to my knees, and I'm going to suck that cock into my mouth."

"And now I want to get hard again, but I think I'm completely spent. You've milked me."

They both visibly shuddered at that word.

"Oh my God, never say that phrase again."

"I am so sorry," Aaron said with a laugh, mock horror on his face. "I don't know what I was thinking. That was a horrible, horrendous thing to say."

"It was. And now we'll have to go find salt and throw it over our shoulders and spin outside twice to make sure it never comes back to haunt us."

"Let's get dressed. We have a bunch of seance shit to do so I don't ruin the evening." Aaron frowned. "What is the plan for the day?"

She swallowed hard, not knowing what to say. She should have talked to him about what had happened with Guy yesterday, but he'd been acting so weird. She had wanted to focus on Aaron, and her, and whatever the hell they were together. She hadn't wanted to think about the fear that had hit her when she was with Guy.

Aaron frowned. "Talk to me. What put that look on your face just now?" He held her close, and she let out a deep breath, needing to inhale his clean scent. Needing to breathe. She knew she shouldn't rely on him so much. Because once she started, it would hurt like hell to walk away. But there was no stopping it right now. Not when she needed to breathe. Needed him.

"Is it your mom? Did she say something after you left with Guy?"

At the sound of Guy's name, Madison shuddered, and Aaron squeezed her harder.

"Talk to me, baby."

"I need to get dressed. I don't want to talk about this naked." She already felt exposed. When Aaron didn't make a joke about her being naked, or him, she knew that she'd worried him. She was anxious herself.

She quickly pulled on a pair of jeans that her mother would never approve of, but they made her happy, as well as a flowy top that was her comfort. Aaron put on jeans as well, and a cotton shirt that molded to his muscles. At any other time, she would have held him close, wanting to feel those muscles through the cotton of his shirt. But she didn't do that now.

Instead, she wrapped her arms around herself, grateful when Aaron came forward and held her close.

"Yesterday, Guy got a little handsy and wouldn't let me go. He got all possessive and weird."

Aaron froze, his whole body going taut as she told him exactly what had happened outside the coffee shop. Aaron took a step back and pulled at her arm. He tugged up her sleeve, the flowy fabric bunching at her elbow, and then he frowned, a scowl covering his face.

"I didn't leave these bruises," he whispered. "I saw the marks on your hips. Those were from me. But these are from him?" he asked, his voice shaking.

She looked down at the palm print. "I didn't even notice. I knew he'd probably hurt me, but I didn't notice."

"I'm going to kill him," he growled.

"No, don't." She reached out, grabbing his arm, and then froze as she noticed that the gesture was the same as Guy had done to her. Aaron cursed under his breath and then gently cupped her face. "You didn't hurt me. You've never hurt me."

"I left bruises on your hips."

"Consensual bruising. You asked me every step of

the way what I wanted, and I did the same to you. Everything we've done has been with our consent."

"Guy bruised you."

"I know," she said, her voice shaking. "And I hate that I couldn't really fight back. He left me almost powerless. The whole point of you and me doing this thing was for me to find my power. And then I just let him—"

He cut her off. "No, you didn't let him do anything. When we get back to Boulder, I'm going to talk with my cousins. They'll be able to tell me exactly who to talk to for some self-defense lessons. I'll take them with you," he added quickly.

"Really?"

"I don't know what I'm doing either, except for play-fighting when I was younger. We'll take classes, learn to defend ourselves, and never feel helpless again. But I'm going to fucking kill him."

"Please, don't. Let's just not talk about him anymore. Or to him. I'll tell my mom what happened, and as long as she doesn't blame me, hopefully, she'll stop with this whole me marrying him thing."

"Why didn't you tell me yesterday?" Aaron asked, his voice low.

"We got distracted," she said, blushing. She had

wanted to be distracted. She hadn't wanted to talk about what'd happened, hadn't wanted it to be real.

But now that she had told Aaron, it felt far too real.

"Okay, I just...I don't know what to do now."

"We're going home," he snapped.

She lifted her head. "I want to go home. I think that's why I put on the jeans."

"Good. We're leaving, and I'm going to go cuddle you and feed you ice cream, and we'll figure out exactly what to do next."

"I thought that maybe you and I would tell my parents everything today," she said, blurting out the words.

He froze.

"You mean about the lie?"

"Well, we're not engaged, but we're sort of...whatever we are. Anyway...I just want to go home."

Thankfully, he didn't bring up exactly what she had just said. She didn't know what he wanted, and she wasn't ready for that conversation, not with so much else on her mind.

Lightning flashed outside, and Aaron frowned, looking out the window as she followed him.

"Fuck, I knew there was a storm coming, but I didn't know it was going to come this fast or be this big."

Neither of them made a penis joke, and that should have told her something.

"I think we should go and find my mother, see what the plans are. We'll have to see if we can even get home in the storm."

Aaron nodded, held her close, and kissed her temple. "Yeah, you're right. Your mom needs to know about Guy. We can tell her about you and me later." The unsaid words were: *once we figure out what we are.*

Madison loved him, that much she knew. But she needed to untangle her thoughts and feelings to see what was best for her, for him, and what would be best for *them.*

She grabbed her bag and slid her fingers into his as they walked out of the room towards the dining area where, hopefully, her mother was just now getting ready for breakfast.

Her mom stood there, her eyes narrowed as she took in the two of them standing together in jeans, looking way too casual for the retreat.

"What do you think you're doing?" her mother asked, her voice pleasant but with an edge.

"We were going to try and head home today," Madison began, "but I don't think the storm is going to let us."

"You can't just leave," her mother snapped. Madison was grateful that nobody was around to hear.

"Yes, we can. We came, we schmoozed, and we can leave. Unfortunately, with this storm, we may be stuck here for another day or so."

"You're so ungrateful," her mother snapped.

"No, I think you are. But this is not the time or the place for this conversation."

"And where did you put Guy? I haven't seen him since your little coffee trip, and I have no idea how it went."

"You mean he didn't report to you?" Madison said, her voice a bit snide even as fear slid over her. Where was Guy? Had he left? Or was he lurking? He was always creeping, something that really hadn't clicked for her until he grabbed her yesterday.

Had he been there solely on her mother's request or because he was just that creepy?

Her mother opened her mouth to say something, but then her dad walked towards them, a scowl on his face. Lightning flashed, and thunder boomed even louder than before, the chandelier above them shaking. And then power snapped off.

A few screams and a couple of gasps could be heard, and Aaron reached out, sliding his arm around her waist.

"Well, that's great," she said.

"Watch your tone," her mother whispered.

Madison almost laughed. They were in the dark with no power, a storm raging outside, and there was no escape.

And, of course, her mother blamed her.

But Madison honestly didn't care. And that was something. Maybe this whole fake fiancé thing had worked. She had stood up to her mother, and she was ready to walk away without a second glance. If only Mother Nature would allow that to happen.

Or maybe Mother Nature was giving her a second chance to find her way with Aaron.

Lightning flashed again, and the wind howled. People started shouting, and then all thoughts of Aaron and what they meant to each other fled as a sense of foreboding crept over her.

The storm was just the beginning.

She knew that much down to her bones.

CHAPTER SEVENTEEN

Aaron cursed under his breath before squeezing Madison's hip and letting her go only to grab her hand and tangle his fingers with hers.

"You okay?" he asked. He looked down at her, the lights from outside barely enough for him to see her face.

"I'm fine. Mom? Dad?"

"We're fine. I cannot believe a place like this doesn't have a backup generator. What are they doing with our money if they're not taking care of us in our time of need?" her mother asked. While Aaron might've thought that the woman was just complaining for the sake of it, he also heard the fear in her voice.

It seemed that when she was scared, she lashed out.

It made sense. Aaron wasn't particularly comfortable right now either with the storm and no power. People started milling around, the large windows on the other side of the room letting in the most light.

"Darling, I'm sure the manager will help us soon. You know Ralph, he's always been a friend of the family."

There was a gruffness to Mark McLard's tone that said he wasn't having fun with this either. Aaron had never understood the couple more. They didn't like things out of their control, hence why they tried to control their daughter. When she fought back, they pushed harder.

Aaron just hated that they'd hurt her along the way.

"Okay, what are we going to do?" Maeve asked, and Aaron blinked, even though they couldn't see him. He wasn't sure she had ever uttered that phrase before in her life. Given how Madison stiffened at his side, he figured she hadn't either.

Very interesting.

The manager came forward, a flashlight in his hand.

"The storm seems to have hit us harder than they predicted," Ralph said. "We apologize. What we're going to do, is get everyone into a central location. My team and I are working on a solution as we speak. It seems that when the tree fell down and knocked out the power lines, it also hit our generator."

Everybody began speaking at once. Aaron made sure that Madison was close to him as others moved in on them to get Ralph's attention.

People talked about refunds, asked about their stuff and other things. Honestly, Aaron could care less. He had Madison at his side, and her parents were near. Everybody that he had a connection to was safe. He was keeping an eye out for Guy, though. Hopefully, the man had already left.

If not?

He'd have to kick the man's ass, storm or no storm.

"Now, if everybody could come to this side of the room, we'll be able to keep track of everybody better. Please don't go off on your own or return to your rooms just yet. We're still waiting on the lights, and we don't want you to get hurt."

"I'm going to sue your ass," somebody growled from behind them. Aaron thought it might have been Joyce's husband.

Dear God, Aaron was with a bunch of people who never had to fend for themselves and clearly lashed out when they were pissed.

This was going to be an interesting night.

"The generator should be up and running soon. Please, come with me."

The storm raged on, the wind howling. Aaron looked down at his phone and cursed when he noticed that there was no signal.

"No signal, no calling out."

"This is the beginning of a horror film," Madison mumbled.

"There's no need to panic," her mother said, sounding as if she were already panicking.

"Maeve, stop rambling," Mark said.

This was a version of hell. An actual hell that Aaron could not escape from.

"I hope it doesn't flood," Madison mumbled.

"We need to throw salt over our shoulder again," he began. "Because if it floods? The whole side of the mountain's coming down. With the dry season and that fire? It's ripe for a mudslide."

He mumbled the words so only Madison could hear. There was no need to start a panic, but he had a feeling that others around him, people with clearer heads, were thinking the same.

The storm wasn't supposed to be this bad. If he had known, he wouldn't have come up here at all. But then again, his head had been in the clouds when it came to Madison, and he hadn't really been paying attention.

Now, someone might get hurt because of that.

"We'll get out of here quickly," he whispered, kissing the top of her head. He kept touching, kissing as if they were a real couple. And maybe they were, but right then, all he could worry about was making sure she was safe.

"Excuse me, Mr. Montgomery?" Ralph asked as he came forward.

"Yes? How can I help?" Aaron asked, wondering why Ralph was singling him out.

"Can I talk to you for a moment?" he asked, gesturing to a corner with fewer people.

Aaron nodded, and Madison walked with him. He didn't mind. He didn't want to leave her alone. Not with the storm, and not with Guy perhaps lurking about.

"Sorry for taking you away from your family."

"My family's right here," he said without thinking, gesturing towards Madison.

She gave him a weird look, one that even he could see despite the dimness of the room, but he forced himself to turn to Ralph and not dwell on the words he had just uttered.

"We could really use your help with the generator."

Aaron frowned. "And how can I help with that?"

"You do work on your furnace, don't you? And you

have a generator for that. My maintenance man is out sick. Honestly, I don't know what I'm doing. I could use a second pair of hands, and you might have noticed, but not everybody here has been out of the office in a while." He whispered the last part so softly that Aaron knew that he didn't want to offend his clientele.

Aaron didn't mind helping. Not at all. He only hoped he could.

"Of course. Let me make sure Madison's safe with her parents, and I'll follow you out."

Relief spread over Ralph's face as lightning flashed again, lighting the room.

A couple of people screamed when the thunder followed, and Aaron shook his head. "We're going to need light in here quick."

"Tell me about it."

"Okay, let's get you over to your mom," Aaron said to Madison.

"I don't need to be held and mothered," Madison whispered.

"I don't know where Guy is. So, yes, I'm going to make sure you're with your parents. You don't have a choice in the matter," he said through gritted teeth. Madison froze, and he cursed under his breath. "I'm sorry, I didn't mean to scare you."

"No, it's the whole storm and potential mudslide

thing. And thinking of everything else. It sort of pushed up in my mind. I need to be alert. Much more than I am. Thank you."

He leaned down and kissed her hard, tugging on her hair just enough to make her part her lips.

"Be safe. I'll be right back."

He told her parents what was going on, and they placed Madison between them as if on guard. He made his way with Ralph to the generator.

Outside, the rain lashed so hard that it slapped at his face, stinging his skin. It was coming down so hard, he was afraid he might bruise, but they kept going.

The wind howled, and they had to shout at each other to get things done. The downpour raged, and lightning arched above them. He worried they might get electrocuted if they weren't careful.

The generator was in a small outbuilding behind the main one, and honestly, he didn't think it was going to be enough to power the whole place.

"Is this it?"

"We've got four more, but the fifth one was damaged beyond repair. And now these are having issues."

"I'll do what I can," Aaron said. "I've got one like this at home. But shit, they're not easy to work with."

"So I've discovered. You can bet your behind I'll be

learning how they work inside and out the next chance I get. Never again will I allow myself to get into this situation."

Aaron liked this Ralph guy. Soon, the two of them were setting up the generators, Aaron's body aching from the exertion.

Going from building to building wasn't easy. Both of them slid in the mud, falling at times, bruising and cutting themselves on jagged rocks.

The rain came down in sheets, and Aaron knew a few trees were already down. There would be no going home tonight.

If they weren't careful, though, the mudslide could be a real thing. He looked up the mountain, trying to see through the storm, but he couldn't tell if anything was forthcoming. The scariest thing was that they would never know until the mud was already there, bringing down half the mountain with it.

He just hoped to hell that didn't happen.

They kept moving, working as a unit until his knuckle's bled, and he was cursing up a blue streak. Finally, however, the low hum of the generators hit his ears, and light filled the building.

"Jesus Christ, thank God."

"Thank Aaron Montgomery," Ralph said with a

laugh, and Aaron snorted, shaking the other man's hand.

"My staff was instructed to keep all people where they were. We're trying to conserve energy, but I have a feeling we'll need to call the authorities for help. The storm is twice as big as I thought it would be. Nobody thought it was going to be like this."

"Seems like," Aaron said. "I need to get back to Madison."

"Of course, you do. Thank you again. I don't know what we would've done without you."

"You would have muddled through. We all figure out things when we need to."

They made their way back, the rain coming down even harder now, the ground beneath them a muddy, slippery mess.

He shook himself before he went in, knowing he probably looked a fright.

A couple of people glared over at them and gave them sneering looks, but they could go fuck themselves. They were safe inside, dry, and now warm with the lights on because Aaron had worked his ass off right alongside Ralph to ensure it.

Aaron couldn't find Madison right away, so he went over to where Maeve and Mark were talking, both of them whispering.

"Where's Madison?" he asked without preamble.

They each gave him a look and then glanced into the corner. A look of shock crossed their faces.

"What?" he asked, his adrenaline pumping.

"She was in the corner. We just left her in the corner. She was feeling lightheaded. Oh my God, where's Madison?" Maeve began, her voice going high-pitched.

Others started to turn towards them, and Aaron did his best to look over everybody's heads, trying to find her.

But he couldn't. There was no sign of her.

"Maybe she went to the restroom. Or back to your room for something," Mark began.

"I'll go check. You go look for her here. And then we'll meet back here in five minutes."

"She's fine. She's fine," Maeve said, repeating the words over and over again. "She wouldn't have gone out in this."

"Did Madison tell you about Guy?" Aaron asked, trying not to panic.

"What do you mean?"

"He hurt her," Aaron growled out.

"What?" Maeve said, her hand going to her throat.

"I'll talk to you about it later. But, yeah, he hurt her.

We need to find Madison right now. She wouldn't have just gone off like this."

"I'm sure she's fine," Mark said, giving Aaron a look. Aaron understood. He didn't want Maeve to panic. And he wouldn't add fuel to the fire.

No, he would simply let all the panic slide through him.

Because while he couldn't fucking find Madison, and it terrified him, she had to be okay.

If she wasn't?

He had no idea what the fuck he would do.

Madison dug her heels into the mud, doing her best to pull away from Guy. He only tugged on her arm harder, nearly ripping her limb from its socket.

"What are you doing? Let me go!" she roared over the din of the pounding rain and thunder.

"Stop fighting. This will all go easier if you come with me." Guy tugged her harder, and she cried out, tears forming. He was so much stronger, and the fact that he had a kitchen knife in his other hand, one that he had threatened to use but hadn't yet, worried her more.

She had been sitting in the corner, trying to see where Aaron was, when someone came around from the blind spot in the room and put their hand over her mouth.

She hadn't had a chance to scream because as soon as she realized that she was being pulled away, it was too late. Guy had her outside almost immediately, the roar of the rain masking any sound that she might have made.

Now, he didn't bother covering her mouth but was practically dragging her down the side of the mountain towards wherever he planned to go.

"Why are you doing this?" she asked, fear crawling over her skin. Nobody was out here to hear her scream, just like before. She didn't know how she was supposed to get out of this. How was she supposed to save herself?

Even if a storm weren't hurting everything and making it already far too dangerous, she wasn't sure they would make it out of this. She wasn't sure *she* would make it out of this.

"Why? Because I have to. You're supposed to marry me. And nothing's going off the way it should."

"What? I'm not going to marry you. This isn't going to work out. If you just let me go, we can forget any of this ever happened."

Guy let out a shocked laugh, only barely audible over the rain.

"You stupid bitch. Fuck you. Your mother promised me your money. Yet you had to go and get with that stupid artist and lie. That blue collar bitch. Who the fuck do you think you are?"

Madison didn't understand Guy's need or desperation. It didn't make any sense to her.

He tugged her under a tree, his chest heaving, and while she wanted to run away, he still had the knife pointed at her. Plus, she was all turned around from the mud and the rain. She couldn't even see the lodge anymore.

She didn't know where they were going, or even if Guy had a plan, but she knew that she wasn't going to make it out of this if she didn't get away soon. She had to make a move. She had to find Aaron. She had to get help.

Aaron was out here somewhere, she reminded herself. Or at least he had been. Maybe he'd find her. But he may not even know that she was gone.

She was going to die out here if she wasn't careful.

She tried not to panic, but the emotion was welling up inside her.

She let out a breath as Guy glared at her. She licked her lips, trying to calm herself so she could think. It wasn't easy when all she wanted to do was scream and fight, but she knew she wasn't strong enough. Not with this man.

She had to find a way out of this.

"So, you wanted to marry me? All of this for marriage?"

"I don't give a shit about you. I need your fucking money. I made a few bad investments, and now the people I owe are sick of waiting. I need what you have to give to them. You were my meal ticket. But then you had to go and grow a spine. All of a sudden. What the fuck? Your mother told me that you would be pliant. That you would do whatever she and I said. That you—and your money—would be mine."

Madison knew that her mother could be cruel sometimes, but she knew those weren't her mother's words. They were all Guy's.

He had twisted her mom's cruelty even more.

Madison had to get away.

She just didn't know how she was supposed to do that, not with the knife he held on her, or the fact that she didn't know where they were on the property.

He tugged on her again, trying to take her down the mountain. She shook her head, pulling back with all her might.

"We're going to die out here. The storm's too bad. We need to go back."

"You bitch," he growled. "You have to come with me. My car's down here."

"It's not safe to drive," she said, trying to make him see reason, even though she knew he wouldn't.

"Stop trying to save yourself. We're going to find someone to marry us, and then I'm taking what is rightfully mine. I had to follow you around like a little lovesick puppy, listening to whatever your dumb ass mother said, and all because I was promised something. And now I'm not getting it? No. I get what I want. I've always gotten what I want. And that means I'm getting you."

He was deranged. He'd lost his fucking mind. She really needed to get away from him.

He tugged her to her feet, wrenching her arm again. But this time, she pulled away, thankful that he slid in the mud as he tried to swipe at her with the knife.

It was pure luck that the move worked, but she ran and kept running, her feet sliding in the mud, the rain slapping at her skin. Hail came, and she knew she was likely bleeding from the little ice pellets battering her skin, but she didn't care. She needed to get to Aaron. Had to get to her mom and dad. She just wanted to be home. Away from Guy.

She kept running up the hill to where she thought the lodge was and prayed she was going in the right direction. She could hear Guy behind her, screaming her name. Her heart raced so fast that she could barely hear anything over the pounding and the rush of blood in her ears.

"Madison!" her mother yelled. Relief and fear filled her. While she knew that her mother had had no part in this, she *had* brought Guy into her life. However, Madison's mother hurt with words, never anything else.

Madison knew that deep down in her soul.

"Mom, get back. He's coming!" She refused to let her mother get hurt by this man. It wasn't her fault that Guy was insane.

"What?" Maeve gasped.

Madison reached out but slipped at the last moment, banging her knee against a rock. Stars burst behind her eyelids, and she sucked in a breath, telling herself that she was going to be okay. She just needed to keep moving. But Guy pulled at her hair, and she fell back again, screaming.

"Guy? What are you doing? Get off my daughter. Is that a knife?"

"You bitch!" Guy screamed. Madison didn't know if he was talking to her or her mom.

"Let go of my daughter!" her mother said, falling slightly as she tried to make her way over.

"Stop. He has a knife!" Her mom's eyes widened,

even as the rain picked up, the wind howling even louder around them.

"Just go, save yourself," Madison yelled.

"Let go of my daughter!" her mother growled, coming straight at Guy.

"Please. Take me instead," she pleaded.

"No! Mom." Madison couldn't believe it. It was like a different person was standing in front of her right now. Or maybe the person that she had known when she was younger.

"Let go of my baby."

Madison tugged at Guy's grip, and both of them went down to their knees as she tried to get away. Guy scrambled for her, pulling at her clothes. The sound of ripping fabric filled the air as she tried to get to her mother.

"Mom, run!"

But it was too late. Guy was there, a rock in his hand. He smashed it against her mother's skull. Her mom's eyes went wide for an instant before blood flowed, and then she crumpled to the ground.

"No!"

Madison turned wobbly in the knees and pushed herself forward in the mud, lunging at Guy, hitting him with all her might. He scrambled back, the knife falling to the ground. She hit him again, pushing at him. Screaming. He yelled, but it was all so incoherent, she couldn't even tell what he was saying anymore. Didn't know if they were words at all. It didn't matter, though. She pushed him again, grateful when he fell back. She moved to her mother, scared of what she would find. Blood seeped from an open wound on her mother's forehead, but she seemed to be breathing. Madison had to get her out of this rain, needed to get her out of this situation and get help. Madison's clothes stuck to her, and blood coated her hands, her knees, and every other place she'd hurt when she fell and from where the hail had hit her. She had a slight cut on her arm from the knife earlier, but she couldn't feel anything. She was far too cold for that.

If they didn't get back to the lodge soon, they were going to die out here. Not necessarily because of Guy, but because of the elements.

She began to drag her mom away, too weak to pick her up. She wasn't sure if she would make it.

Suddenly, Guy was there, screaming again. He pushed her mother away from her, and then wrapped his hands around Madison's throat.

She clutched at Guy's hands, digging her fingernails into his skin.

She gasped, trying to breathe, but he squeezed harder. Madison fell to her knees beside her mother, tears rolling down her face and mixing with the rain.

This was it. She was going to die. Her mother had actually tried to save her, but it hadn't been enough.

They were going to die together, with nobody to hear them scream for help.

Suddenly, someone else was there, and Guy was on the ground with a large shape on top of him, the person punching and yelling.

Madison coughed, her gaze spotty as she tried to fight for breath. She looked up to see Aaron pummeling Guy's face. The man she loved was enraged. He shook, his body covered in mud, and so wet from the rain that it looked as if he had jumped into a pool.

"Aaron!" she gasped, crying fully now, her body shaking with wracked sobs.

Aaron gave one last hard punch, knocking the other man out, then scrambled off Guy and came to her. He cupped her face, his gaze searching hers.

"Madison. Are you okay?"

"My mom," she choked out, not able to say anything else.

He looked down at the blood on her, and then over at her mom. His face went impossibly pale.

"Ralph! Mark! They're here. Get the authorities!" he yelled over her head before pulling Madison close and going down to his knees to check her mom's neck for a pulse. When he gave her a tight nod, tears flowed harder, and she just clung to him, shaking.

The earth started to rumble, and she looked up to see mud coming at them.

"Oh my God," she whispered.

"Come on, get them out of here." Aaron kissed her hard and then handed her over to her father, who helped her stand. Aaron moved ahead, her mother held close to his chest, carrying her up as if she weighed nothing.

"I've got this asshole," Ralph growled, putting Guy in a fireman's carry as the mud, trees, branches, rocks, and everything else came at them. The mudslide happened faster than anything she'd ever seen in her life.

"We need to hurry!" Aaron shouted over the deafening noise.

"Guy had a knife," she said, clutching her father's chest. He practically dragged her up the hill on the other side of where the mudslide was coming from.

There was a ravine between the two edges. As long as they made it to higher ground, they should be fine, as would the lodge. But if they'd remained where they were before Aaron had come, they likely would have died.

If Aaron hadn't come for her, that would've been it.

She shook, the adrenaline pumping through her at a fast pace. She knew she was going to crash at any minute.

"Daddy," she whispered in shock.

"Let's get you inside. Let's get your mother and you inside. Come on, pumpkin."

He held her close, and she looked over at Aaron, knowing that he had only let her father hold her so he could carry her unconscious mother up the hill. No one else would have been strong enough. As it was, Ralph was struggling with Guy's weight, but she didn't care. At this point, Guy could be left behind. But then again, she didn't want that death on her conscience.

They made their way to the top of the hill, the mudslide roaring on the other side of the small ravine, and then people were all talking at once, coming at them. Lights flashed, and she realized that the authorities had arrived.

She wasn't exactly sure what would happen next. The paramedics came towards her mother, and Aaron handed her off to them before turning and facing her. Madison didn't know what to say. She simply threw herself at him, pulling away from her father and sinking into Aaron's hold.

He had saved her. Had saved her mother.

And all she wanted to do was hold him.

And never let go.

CHAPTER NINETEEN

Aaron leaned against the wall, grateful that the authorities were leaving. The cops had taken Guy away in handcuffs. He had woken soon after they landed in the lodge, with Ralph hogtying the man just in case the police didn't bring their restraints.

Aaron liked Ralph. He couldn't help it. He knew that, no matter what, he would end up being friends with the lodge manager.

The night's events weren't exactly how he'd thought to spend his evening, but then again, nothing about his life was normal.

Not anymore.

He looked over at Madison, saw how she and her

family talked to one another, standing so close it was as if they had never been on opposite sides of a fight.

Her mother had woken up as soon as they got her dry. Though the paramedics were sure she had a concussion and would need stitches, they planned to wait a little longer before they put her in the ambulance and took her away. Primarily because the storm had washed out some of the roads, and she was safe and being watched—mostly by Madison, who seemed to never want her mother out of her sight.

After everything that had happened, somehow, this had been the rallying point that had brought them back together. Maeve was like a completely different person, and Aaron didn't think it was the knock on the head that had done it. No, it was almost losing her daughter. It was as if that scare had changed everything.

He didn't know if things would stay this way, but he had a feeling that Madison would do her best to make sure they did.

Somehow, she had found her family again, and he was now only an observer, not sure what to say.

She didn't seem to need him anymore. And, honestly, he wasn't sure what he would have done if he had lost her. And that scared him. But she needed to be with her family right now, he knew that much. Maybe that meant it would be best to walk away soon.

He just didn't know if he was strong enough to do that.

The cops had questioned him, looked at the bruises on his hands and his bloody knuckles, and hadn't said a damn thing. Instead, they'd looked almost...proud of him. He'd take that. He had almost been too late to save Madison. Almost too late to save the person he loved more than anything.

And because he loved her, he was going to do whatever was best for her, even if that wasn't what was best for him.

Mark came up to him then, a frown on his face. Aaron rolled his shoulders back and looked at the older man.

"Mr. McClard."

"Call me Mark. You saved my girls. I'm never going to be able to thank you enough."

Aaron shook his head. "You don't need to thank me. If we had told you about Guy to begin with, maybe this wouldn't have happened."

"There are a lot of *shoulds* and questions about what would've happened. Things we need to talk about as a family. But I want to thank you for being there for my ladies, for saving them. I'm glad you're with our baby girl. Even if it was a lie at first, I can see it's the truth now."

Mark held out his hand, and Aaron blinked, not knowing what to say. He just reached out and clasped it.

"I'm glad I was there."

"So am I. I'll be proud to have you as part of our family." Mark squeezed Aaron's hand before going back to his wife. It looked like they would be putting her in the ambulance soon, which meant that Madison would likely be leaving. That also meant it was time for Aaron to let her go.

Madison came over, and he let out a breath, doing his best not to look like he was breaking inside. "I'm going with Mom, and Dad's going to follow in the car. I hope that's okay. I know I came up here with you, but I don't think I can let her out of my sight."

Aaron reached out and tucked a piece of hair behind her ear. "I understand. You need to go with your mom. You need to be with her for this. She came out to save you."

Tears filled her eyes, and he felt like a heel for bringing that up.

"She did. It was like she was my mom again. I know we have a lot to talk about. All of us. But I'm just so happy she's okay. That you're okay. That you were here."

He swallowed hard.

If he were a smart man, he would tell her how he felt. He would say that he loved her and that he always would. But he wasn't a smart man. He knew exactly what she needed, and it wasn't him.

"You're going to be healing as a family. And you need each other. It'll be good for you to be with them."

"It will," she said, confusion on her face. She frowned up at him. "What's wrong?

"I guess it's over."

Why did his voice sound so icy? Why was the rest of him cold, as well?

Her eyes widened. "What?

"There's no more engagement. There's no more Guy. You don't need me to be your beard anymore or anything like that. You have your family. You need to be with them. They see you now. For who you really are."

Just like I saw you.

She didn't say anything, but he didn't really let her. Instead, he leaned down and brushed his lips across hers, a goodbye that he knew would break him. But he didn't care.

He leaned away and gestured towards her mother. "They're going to be taking her away soon. You don't want to miss it. I'm glad I was here this weekend. I'm glad that I got to know you."

She just looked at him, seeming stunned, but still didn't say anything.

He was an asshole for even doing this, but it would be a good break. It would make things easier and allow her to figure out exactly what she wanted without him.

She finally had her family. He didn't need to be a part of it.

"Madison, we're heading out," her father said. Madison just shook her head at Aaron.

"Go. It's what you need."

She had a bandage on her head, another on her arm, and he couldn't look at any of it anymore. She needed to go, or he was going to break.

Even more than he already was.

Instead of saying anything, she simply walked away, leaving him alone. Just like he wanted.

He knew it was for the best. She had a second chance with her family. And there was no reason for them to yearn for what they couldn't have, not with what anything they might have shared had begun with a lie.

He knew that. And one day, he'd let himself truly believe it.

CHAPTER TWENTY

Madison poured herself a cup of tea after doing the same for her mother. Maeve McClard sat draped on the comfortable white settee near the two-story-tall windows, framed perfectly and looking elegant in the light. Yet her mother wore no makeup, and her hair was in a braid down her back.

Madison had never once seen her mother like this. Not since she was a little girl. Even on Christmas morning, her mother wore full makeup and had perfectly done hair for photos.

Madison hadn't minded at all. She had a few friends who enjoyed wearing makeup, as well. Some even did it for a living so they liked to be their version of presentable at all times. Her mother had always taken that a bit to the extreme, so Madison had never been able to see beneath the exterior.

"Here you go," Madison said, handing over the delicate china cup and saucer.

Her mother smiled, nodding slightly. "Thank you, darling." She leaned over the cup, closing her eyes as she inhaled. "I love this hibiscus blend. I never sit down and just drink tea anymore."

Madison took a seat in the armchair next to the settee and inhaled her tea's floral scent. "I don't normally either. Mostly because I deal with coffee and cupcakes."

She nearly winced at bringing up her job, a sore subject for them both. But it was her mother who winced this time.

If her mom said something about her job, Madison might leave. She had learned that life was far too short to lay down and take anything that hurt anymore.

She was still trying to figure out exactly what was going on in her family now, and how they were going to move past the pain and terror of the past. But she wasn't going to sit back and get hurt anymore, no matter what.

At least, that's what she told herself.

"I really should try some of your coffee sometime."

Madison blinked and set her cup and saucer on the antique table beside her.

"Oh?"

Her mother gave her a sad smile and shook her head, taking a sip of her tea before doing her best to place it next Madison's. Madison stood up, took the cup from her, and set it down so her mother didn't have to stretch.

It had only been a couple of days since the attack, and her mom was still dealing with the aftereffects of the concussion. Madison's own stitches had ached that morning, but she would never forget the sight of her mother crumpling to the ground after Guy hit her.

That visual would haunt her forever.

Just as Aaron's parting words would. She pushed those thoughts from her mind, not wanting to think about him right now. She wasn't sure if she could ever think about him again.

At least not without dying a little inside.

"I have not been a good mother recently," her mom said, shocking Madison out of her reverie.

"Oh?"

Her mother snorted and then rubbed her temple.

"I deserved that. I deserved that, and so much more. But, Madison, I have always wanted what was best for you."

"I know that. It's just...I don't think you went about it in the best ways." She was trying to be as delicate as she could but calling her mother out on being a bitch wasn't what she should be doing.

"You are too kind. Maybe that was the problem. You've always been so nice to me, even when I was terrible. I wanted you to have the best. To have the best life, family, work. So, when I got scared that I wasn't doing well enough as your mother, I got these thoughts in my head that I had to force you into situations so you could become the perfect McClard."

"There's no such thing as perfection, Mother."

"Oh, I've learned." Her mother winced as Madison's eyes widened. "I did not mean that you weren't perfect. I meant the idea of perfection is ridiculous. I put all these expectations on you because I didn't know how to help you. When in reality, you didn't need my help. You are a beautiful woman, one with great business sense, and you have so much. Sadly, I didn't see any of it because I was blinded by the fact that you didn't do it my way."

"I didn't." Madison didn't apologize for that, and she refused to. A few kind words now wouldn't make up for everything her mother had done in the past. But it would be cruel of Madison to not do her best to at least accept the apology. They had to meet somewhere in the middle, or there would be no healing the bridges that had been burned.

"I am trying to learn to be a better person. It took almost losing you to realize what I had become. I know that my words today, me saying that I'm sorry, won't fix that. But I hope you will give me a chance to find a way to make things better. I have a long road to recovery, to figuring out exactly how I'm going to do what I need to do. But I hope you'll let me try to make up for the kind of person I've been. For the person I am," she corrected.

"Your mother is speaking for both of us," her father said as he came into the room, a mug of coffee in his hand.

"Come sit next to me, darling," her mother said, patting the seat next to her. Her parents rarely touched in front of her. They didn't even sit next to each other most times. So the fact that her father sat down next to her mother and squeezed her hand while kissing her temple, told Madison that things far beneath the surface had been broken for her parents. Things that had nothing to do with her. Maybe this wake-up call would be good for everybody. She just hoped that when the bruises healed, the ashes that remained didn't blow away in the wind.

"I'm sorry for everything. I'm going to try not to be such a lackluster father."

"You guys weren't horrible parents." Madison paused. "At least you didn't start out that way."

"Ouch," her father said with a laugh. "We deserved that."

And more.

"I don't know how I got this way," her mother said. "And it's not just the concussion talking," she added. Madison snorted.

"Well, I hope not," she said. "Because once you're back to a hundred percent, I really hope we can find a way to fix what's been broken over time in our family. Because I want you to get to know me as I am now, not as the woman you thought I needed to be. And I hope you'll want to stay this person that you've become," she whispered.

"I don't think that a single knock on the head is what changed this," her mother said, her voice soft. "Seeing you out there with blood and mud all over you? And it being all because of Guy? I'm not sure where I went wrong. I mean, I understand the beginnings of it, but how could I not see him for what he was?"

Her father held her mother's hand, and Madison let out a breath. "I didn't see it either."

"You saw more than we did," her father admonished.

"Perhaps I did, but I didn't realize he could change so drastically. I always thought he was suave, I didn't realize it was a layer of the exterior that hid the cruelty beneath."

"He's going to jail for a long time. We will make sure of that," her father said, his voice stern.

She trusted her father to deal with the legal issues because that's what he did. He cleaned up messes, and he used his power. This once, she was happy that he had that ability. Because she never wanted to see Guy again. As it was, she saw him in her nightmares, and she didn't even want that anymore.

"I haven't seen Aaron here," her mother said out of the blue, and Madison blinked.

"Oh, well, you know..."

"That it was a fake engagement?" her mother asked, her eyes filled with light for the first time since the attack. "I knew that, but I also saw the way you two were with each other. It didn't end up being a lie in the end, did it?"

Madison swallowed hard and looked down at the engagement ring she still wore, the one that reminded her of him so much. He had texted to ensure that she was safe and home, but he hadn't contacted her outside of that. Lincoln and the others had called, and Lincoln had even come by with Ethan and Holland. But no one mentioned Aaron. The lack of his name on their lips was a crack in the marble of the shell she'd made herself. The evidence of them knowing not to bring him up told her that Aaron wanted nothing more to do with her. And she hated that she was breaking inside because of it.

"We're no longer together," she said after a moment, the silence deafening.

"I'm so sorry," her mother whispered.

"Really?" she asked and could have kicked herself. They were having such a good day. And here she was, being rude.

"Really. Aaron was good for you." Her mother shook her head as Madison opened her mouth to speak. "I'm sorry I didn't see that sooner. And I'm sorry I tried to use his popularity in his work as a notion that he'd help you instead of being good for you for who he was. I'm trying not to be a horrible person, and it's going to take me a long time to get over my preconceived notions."

"Your mother is not the only one who has to get over some issues," her father said.

"I'm really glad to hear that from both of you. But Aaron and I are no longer together."

"Yet you still wear his ring," her mother said. It felt like it should hurt, but it didn't. She was too numb.

"I think I'm just too tired to take it off," she lied.

Her mother and father each gave her a knowing look, and then they changed the subject to cupcakes. They talked about her work and unimportant things, and yet she felt as if they were getting to know each other for the first time.

The bash on the head hadn't changed everything. It was them nearly losing each other. And Madison knew that there would be setbacks, there was more work to be done, but this was a step in the right direction. She couldn't keep moving backward. Even if going in that direction meant going towards Aaron.

She didn't have him anymore. He had walked away to give her space, and it had been so abrupt, she hadn't really processed it yet. She hadn't been able to tell him how she felt, and she was afraid that once she did, *if* she did, she'd just end up even more bruised.

But she wasn't the same person she had been when all of this started. When she paced in the parking lot and felt like she was screwing everything up. She wasn't the same person who had gone to the art show.

She wasn't even the same woman she had been when they kissed for the first time.

Perhaps that had to count for something. Only she wasn't sure it did or what it meant. Not when she felt like she was losing everything.

Or as if she hadn't been worth it to begin with.

CHAPTER TWENTY-ONE

Aaron had expected the pounding on the door. Had anticipated the shouting.

He hadn't seen the fist to the face coming.

Or perhaps he had, just not from who threw it.

"Ethan, what the hell?" Lincoln snapped from his lover's side.

Aaron rubbed his jaw and grinned at his little brother.

"I thought Lincoln was going to hit me. And I would have let him. I wasn't expecting you to do it."

"Well, I didn't want Lincoln to hit you because that might hurt Madison's feelings. She doesn't like it when people stand up for her like that. But if I do it, it's just a brother to brother thing. So, what the fuck, Aaron? Why is Madison crying in her home all alone while you're here acting like an asshole?"

Aaron felt as if he'd been doused in water. He took a few steps back, bile rising to his throat.

"Now that you got that out of your system, darling, let's go inside. We can kick his ass properly," Lincoln said through gritted teeth. Aaron took a few steps back so both of them could walk through the door, each of them glaring.

"It wasn't real," Aaron began, but Lincoln held up a hand.

"No, we're not going to start with that. We're going to start with this." And then Lincoln held out his arms and hugged Aaron so tight, he could barely breathe.

"Thank you for saving my family. Fuck. I can't believe I almost lost them."

Aaron could hear the tears in the other man's voice, and he swallowed hard to keep his own at bay and just hugged the other man back. Then Ethan walked up, embracing them both. The three of them stood there, just breathing as they held onto one another. Aaron wondered how he had gotten himself into this situation. Not being held by his brother and friend, but that they needed to comfort him at all.

"That's enough of that," Ethan said, tugging Lincoln away. He's mine," his brother said with a wink, and Aaron laughed. This was the first time he had truly laughed since he watched Madison walk away when he told her to go.

"Lincoln is pretty, but he's not my type."

"I'm everybody's type, thank you very much," Lincoln said, but the humor rang false.

"I'm sorry," Aaron said.

"You really shouldn't be apologizing to me. You should be apologizing to the woman you hurt."

"It wasn't real," Aaron whispered again.

"Oh, fuck that. We all know it's real. You might've started out with this joke or ruse to give her some space, but I saw how you two were with each other. And don't tell me you two weren't sleeping together, because that would be a big fucking lie," Lincoln growled.

Aaron ran his hand through his hair and noticed that he needed a haircut. But he didn't care. He was too tired. Too exhausted to work, to create. He felt like he was doing everything wrong.

He deserved being yelled at, though. He deserved it so much. But he wasn't right for Madison. She needed space, and him not giving it to her would only hurt her in the end.

"She needs time to be with her family."

"You're right. But not all the time. Jesus Christ, you need to save her from herself."

Aaron narrowed his eyes at Ethan. "What do you mean?"

"All I'm saying is that the two of you were great together. And I don't care if you thought you weren't dating, you were. So don't even start with that."

"Madison needs you, too. You guys *were* good together," Lincoln said. "And considering that I want my precious baby cousin pure and perfect, the fact that I'm even allowing this to happen should tell you how good I think you two were."

"I'm not going to touch on that subject, if that's okay with you," Aaron said, thinking of all the kinky shit they had done.

Lincoln narrowed his eyes. "Yes, let's not."

"I walked away to give her space. Hell, to give *me* space. Everything happened so fast. I didn't know what was real and what was fake anymore."

"Then talk to her," Ethan said.

"That's funny, considering what happened to you," Aaron said, regretting the words as soon as he spoke them.

"You're right," Ethan said. "I almost ruined everything."

"Same here," Lincoln said.

"You know what we did?" Ethan said.

"We fucking talked to one another after the rest of you guys yelled at us," Lincoln finished.

"So, here we are," Ethan said.

"Yelling at you," Lincoln added.

"Okay, I get it. What if she says no? What if she's healing and not sad at all that I'm gone?"

"What if you're a fucking idiot?" Lincoln countered.

"Nice, honey," Ethan drawled.

"I miss her so much," Aaron said, running his hand over his beard. "I didn't want what we had to get confused and jumbled in the charade. And now I don't know how to go back."

"You just go back," Ethan whispered. "And you grovel. You beg. And you tell her exactly how you feel."

"But first..." Lincoln said.

"I should shower?" Aaron drawled.

"Okay, yes. First, you should shower. But then? You should figure out exactly what you want. Because you don't get a second chance," Lincoln said. "This is all part of your first chance. But if you walk away again? If you hurt her? There'll be no place on this Earth you can hide from me." Lincoln glared.

"Figure out what you want," Lincoln repeated.

"I already know what I want," Aaron said, looking

down at his hands. The hands that had touched her. That still craved her.

"And?" Ethan prompted.

"I want her."

"Then go get her. Grovel your heart out. And don't fuck it up," Lincoln said.

"How the hell do I grovel?" Aaron asked.

Ethan threw his hands up into the air. "You read how many romance novels? Read one of your precious books and learn how to grovel. And do it well. There'd better be glass on the floor for you to walk over at this point."

"It's crawling, darling," Lincoln said, laughing. "Seriously, though. Crawl over glass. That'll help."

"But don't get too much blood on the carpet," Ethan countered.

"I don't know if you guys are helping at all," Aaron said with a laugh.

"You know we are. Now, pick up a book, take a shower, but don't bring the book into the shower because you'll ruin it. And then go grovel. Tell her how you feel. Just make sure you know what that is first."

Aaron sighed and nodded, knowing they were right.

He already knew what he wanted. Knew what he felt for Madison McClard.

He loved her.

And now he needed to figure out how to tell her so she didn't kill him.

Far easier said than done.

CHAPTER TWENTY-TWO

I n the five days since she had been kidnapped, almost murdered, almost wed, and nearly fell down a mountain with a deranged psychopath, Madison felt as if she had finally come into her own. She was closing up the shop for the day, wanting some time alone. She'd sent Brynn home after the other woman did nothing but hover the entire time she was in the kitchen.

Madison loved Brynn. She adored the fact that Brynn had stepped up to take over Sin in a Cup for the days that Madison had been off, but she needed some space.

Of course, that phrase just reminded her of Aaron. She growled, angry now that he dared to walk away.

Tomorrow, she told herself. She would confront him

tomorrow and tell him exactly what she felt. And then she'd tell him to go fuck himself if he tried to push her away again.

She was still a bit achy, not only in her body but also in her heart. She *was* feeling better, though.

Guy had already taken a plea deal, so she wouldn't have to see him again if she didn't want to. She knew the specifics but didn't want to focus on them because he didn't matter. He was a blip in the emotional turmoil she was already in.

But she had her shop, she had her coffee, and she had her cupcakes.

She looked down at the chain she wore around her neck, wondering why she had even put it on.

She didn't have Aaron, but she had a piece of him. Tomorrow, when she went to yell at him, or maybe just to ask him why he walked away, thus forcing her to walk away from him, she'd ask what he wanted to do with the ring. The symbol that had started out as a lie but had come to mean so much to her.

She had never once thought they were engaged, but perhaps they had been starting something. A relationship? She needed those labels, but regardless, she had thought they'd shared more than just a deception.

She had let Aaron inside her heart. Inside her body. And she knew that he was scared. Had pushed her away for a reason. Now, she needed to know what those reasons were.

Someone knocked on the door, and she looked up, freezing.

She had closed all the shades except for the glass panes at the front, so nobody could see in unless they were at the door, straining to see her sweeping up the final remnants of the day.

She had allowed herself to be alone in the building when she might've been scared before. But she knew she was safe because she did her best to stay locked in, and Guy wasn't around anymore.

She would not let fear rule her.

Yet she nearly screamed at the sight of Aaron standing at the front door. And here she was, holding a broom and looking down at the ring in her hand.

She let the chain drop to her chest and moved towards him on shaky legs.

Should she open the door? Or should she just walk away and pretend that he wasn't there?

No, that would be running. And she'd already told herself that she was going to see him tomorrow.

She might as well get it over with now.

Might as well break.

But she wouldn't.

Not again.

She let out a breath and approached the door. Unlocking it, she met his gaze.

"Hi," she whispered. He swallowed hard, and her gaze went straight to the long lines of his throat.

"Thank you for opening the door. I wasn't sure you would."

She looked up at him and frowned. "I wasn't sure I was going to either for a moment."

"Can I come in? Or…I can stand right here. I don't want you to feel like I'm crowding you."

"Come in. Let's talk. We need to. And I want to make sure the door's closed and locked."

He frowned as he looked around, likely noticing that the chairs were on the tables and the lights were off.

"Are you alone here?"

She nearly rolled her eyes but understood where he was coming from.

"Brynn just left. And, yes. I'm alone. And my car is parked in the garage, not out in the alley. I'm being safe."

"I don't like that you're alone."

"You don't get to have an opinion on what I do, do you?" she asked, not realizing that she was going to snap the words until she'd said them.

Aaron stuffed his hands into his pockets and nodded. "I guess I deserve that."

"No, I don't want to hurt you. I don't want to yell. I'm just so tired of yelling."

"I'm tired of yelling, too. Though I haven't been the one doing the yelling. Your cousin did most of that. And my brother."

Her eyes widened. "Wait, is that a bruise on your chin? Did Lincoln hit you?" She reached out and brushed her fingers along his newly shaven jaw, her eyes going wide. "I cannot believe he hit you."

"He didn't. Ethan did."

Her hand fell, and she blinked, sure she hadn't heard correctly. "Ethan? Sweet baby Ethan?"

Aaron snorted and shook his head. "I'm going to have to use that phrase with him, I think. I've never actually heard someone call him sweet baby anything."

"I know he's your older brother, but he always seems so innocent and sweet."

"And I was never innocent?" he teased. It felt like they were back to their old selves. Madison had missed it. Even though the crack across her heart still burned.

"There's nothing innocent about you, and we both know it," she said, sounding far more sultry than intended.

He licked his lips, and she bit hers.

"Why are you here, Aaron? If it's to check up on me, I'm fine. I'm working. I'm making do. Guy isn't here. He can't be."

Aaron reached out as if to touch her face but seemed to think better of it at the last minute, letting his hand fall. She felt a bit bereft at the lack of touch. She needed him.

And she hated herself for wanting that touch, for wanting *him* so much.

"I'm an idiot," he said, shocking her out of her thoughts.

"You are, but why?" she asked. He laughed, bringing a smile to her lips.

"Again, I deserve that. I'm an idiot for pushing you away. I thought you needed time with your family. I thought you just needed space to breathe and figure out what you wanted. Because I assumed, I hurt you and myself, thinking you didn't need me. But you know what we didn't do?"

"What?" she breathed.

"We didn't fucking talk about how I felt. How we felt. What the hell were we thinking?"

"It's hard to open up to people."

"I know. And when I read about those couples in books that don't talk about what they're feeling, I scream at them and tug at my hair, begging them to just say what's on their minds. And then I realized it's hard. To open yourself up like that? It's fucking hard. To tell somebody what you feel, knowing that they may not feel the same and could hurt you with just a word."

"I know," she said, her heart beating fast in her ears. She didn't know where he was going with this, but she knew if he didn't get to the point quickly, she would either thrash him or profess her love.

Oh God, how did she get into this situation?

She looked at Aaron Montgomery and suddenly knew that she had fallen in love with him the second he announced that he was her fiancé.

In that moment of panic and confusion, she had fallen hard for him. And she hadn't even realized it.

"Then why did you push me away?" she asked, whispering the words.

"I thought you needed time with your mom. Honestly, that was the main part." He ran his hands through his hair, and she wanted to do the same. Wanted to reach out and touch him. But she didn't. She couldn't invite the hurt again. Not until they spoke.

"And I was so afraid that if you realized the charade didn't need to continue, you would walk away first. That you would figure out that I didn't need to be your fake fiancé anymore, and we would move on and just continue being friends. I didn't want that, so I pushed you away first. I'm so fucking sorry."

Madison blinked, surprised that he was so honest, and yet she shouldn't have been.

"Aaron. You didn't need to push me away. Although I think I'm glad you did."

He blinked. "Really?"

"You're right. It did give me time to talk with my parents and figure out that relationship and just breathe. But I also think if you and I had been able to do it together, I wouldn't be feeling like this now."

"And how do you feel?"

"I'm so angry!" She hadn't meant to say the words, let alone as vehemently as she had, but now that they were out, she couldn't stop them. "I'm angry that my mother put me in this situation. I'm angry that Guy did what he did. I'm angry that I didn't have any control over that. I'm devastated as well as angry that you let me walk away and forced me to do so. And I'm so pissed off that I was the one who walked away. And that I listened. I know it had to do with the shock and just wanting to make sure that my mother was okay after the concussion and everything, but I walked away when you told me to. After doing everything I did to ensure that others knew I could make my own decisions and choices, I followed your lead. I can't believe I did that."

Aaron shook his head and took a step forward. When his hands were on her face, he rested his forehead against hers, and she took a deep breath, inhaling his scent. Needing him to be close.

"I shouldn't have pushed."

"And I shouldn't have listened."

"Now what?" she whispered.

"Now, you're going to listen. I hope you believe me when I tell you that I'm so fucking sorry. And when I tell you exactly how I feel."

"And how do you feel?" she asked, her breath hitching.

"I love you so much, Madison. I don't know when it started, but now, I don't remember a time when you weren't part of my life. Or that I didn't want you to be there. You make me so happy. You make me want to create. You make me want to be a better person. And I walked away, and I shouldn't have. You might've been the one to turn, but I forced it. I walked away long before you did."

Tears filled her eyes. When he wiped them away with his thumbs, she hiccupped a little sob. "I love you, too. I was so afraid that you weren't going to love me back, so I hid it. I put everything into just being you and me and pretending that we made sense and weren't making terrible decisions. Because of that, I didn't let myself desire anything more. But I do. I want it all."

Aaron kissed her then, and she let out a breath, sinking into him, craving his taste. She felt like she was finally home.

"Please forgive me," he whispered. "Forgive me for being an asshole and for taking the decision from your hands. For hurting you. Forgive me."

She pulled away from him slightly and then wiped the tears from his face. "Of course, I do. Though you have to be the one who forgives *me* for walking away."

"We're starting from scratch. You and me."

"I don't think we can go back that far," she said honestly, smiling through her tears.

When he kissed her again, long and hard, she ached for him, needing him. But when he dropped to one knee, she froze, her whole body shaking.

"Aaron," she whispered.

"Madison McClard, I love you. I want to be in your life, and I want to see who we become together. You might still be my fake fiancé, and since you're still wearing my ring, I have a question for you."

"Aaron, I don't think—"

He cut her off.

"Will you date me?" he asked and winked.

She stared at him and then threw her head back and laughed, knowing that this was the most perfect thing he could've said. She wasn't ready to get married. Wasn't prepared for that happily ever after yet.

But she nodded, tears falling down her cheeks, and then she fell to her knees in front of him, kissing him hard.

"Yes, I'll date you."

"Nice. I can't wait to tell everybody that my fiancée is now my girlfriend," he whispered against her mouth. She laughed again, holding him, knowing that they had a long road to travel, but it was one they would traverse together.

Because this was their beginning.

She had been well and thoroughly seduced by Aaron Montgomery.

And yet, she knew they had far more nights to go: one moment and promise at a time.

EPILOGUE

Aaron Montgomery desperately wanted cheese. He wrapped his arms around his girlfriend's waist and nibbled on her neck, and knew that if he played his cards right, he'd be getting it.

"I don't know if you're kissing me because you want to be all lovey-dovey. Or if it's because I have four kinds of cheese on my plate right now."

Aaron laughed, kissed her neck, and then reached around for a white-cheddar-topped cracker. Madison turned in his arms, rolling her eyes.

"I see. So am I ranked above or below the cheese? I just need to know my place."

He swallowed hard, took the champagne glass from her hand, and gulped half of the contents down so he could speak.

"I don't know if you want the answer to that," he said. She pushed at him with her elbow, laughing.

"You are a terrible human being. You're lucky I love you."

He kissed her on the mouth, laughing as she shoved at him with her elbow again.

"I got all of this cheese for us to share, so don't you dare eat it all," she growled at him.

"I promise, I'll share." He took the plate from her, and she widened her eyes at him, looking astonished before he took a toasted piece of bread topped with brie and put it directly into her open mouth.

She closed her eyes as she started to chew, moaning.

That sound went straight to his dick, and he had to swallow hard.

After all, she had moaned like that the hour before they showed up. With her mouth on his cock and his head between her legs, they'd had their appetizer before they even left the house.

He knew there was probably another joke some-where in there, but he didn't care. All he wanted was to kiss his girlfriend again, the same one that still wore her engagement ring, though on her right hand instead of her left.

One day, she would move it to her left hand when

they were ready. And when he asked her properly, when it wasn't part of a plan for deception.

He liked that she still wore it. He had a similar band on his right hand.

After all, he was just as claimed as she was.

"Are you guys going to make out the entire time?" Annabelle asked from his side. He grinned over at his cousin.

"Maybe," he said. "You got a problem with that?"

Annabelle sighed. "How are we the single ones here?"

She looked over at her brother, Benjamin, who shrugged.

"I don't know, but with the way they're all acting all lovey-dovey and swoony, do we *want* to be like them?"

Annabelle looked a bit forlorn for a moment, and Aaron had to wonder what that meant. But then she shook her head. "No, I think we're all just fine being in Fort Collins and happily single without being all weird and mushy."

"You know those are likely famous last words," his cousin from Denver said. He looked over at Maya—looking radiant as always with her ink and piercings—and saw how she stood between her two men. She had a glow about her that said that she was happily in love and settled into her marriage with her two men while raising their babies.

"I think we're doing just fine without a happily ever after. Without a ball and chain," Benjamin said.

Aaron winced. "Oh, no. Don't call a woman that. Or a man. Anyone. Ever. That just gets you into trouble."

One of Maya's husband's snorted. "Yes, and then you end up sleeping on the couch, not even in the guestroom. The couch. With a puny blanket and no pillow."

"Damn straight," Maya said, laughing.

"What are we doing over here?" his mother asked as she came up, kissing everybody on the cheek. His father was right behind her, grinning like a fool.

His parents were proud as punch tonight, and Aaron couldn't blame them.

He and Lincoln had decided to do an art show together, reminiscent of what Lincoln had done all those months ago. This time, however, it showcased both of them.

They had almost gotten Liam to do a reading and Bristol to play something for them, but they both had said no—very firmly, in fact.

He just laughed, knowing that if Madison and his mother had their way, there would be time for that later.

"We were just discussing who would be next to find their spouse," Maya said.

"Well, as soon as all of my ducklings are finally through their weddings, I'm sure I can talk to my sister-in-law and get on that," his mother said. Annabelle and Benjamin shared a look and then grimaced.

"Please do not get her started," Annabelle pleaded.

"I will do no such thing. I've always wanted my babies married and having babies, and now...look at us. You're all happy and thrilled and showing off your talents to the world. I could not be prouder."

His mother dabbed at her eyes with his father's handkerchief, and Aaron barely resisted the urge to roll his. Instead, he kissed Madison's temple and leaned into her as his siblings circled them, joining in on the conversation.

Somehow, each of them had found their happiness when and where they were least expecting it.

Liam and Arden leaned into one another sharing a sly secret between them. It was one that Aaron knew only because he had forced it out of Arden, but he knew the rest would learn soon enough.

Ethan, Holland, and Lincoln each grinned at one another, sharing another secret that he knew would be revealed soon.

Marcus and Bristol looked blissful as they joked with Annabelle and Benjamin about something.

Even Bristol's ex Zia had shown up with her girlfriend Meredith, the two looking like models right off the catwalk.

He had even seen Madison give them a second glance, and that made Aaron even hotter. He couldn't wait to tease her about it later in bed.

There was even a new triad in the group, Ethan's and Marcus's friends from work, who were now together with a third. He was very interested in hearing that story. Maybe one day at another barbecue, Ronin would explain exactly how he'd ended up in bliss with two others.

Nobody batted an eye in this family when it came to triads, so they were in safe company.

Everybody looked happy, except for maybe Annabelle and Benjamin, but Aaron didn't know all their secrets. After all, the Fort Collins cousins were the most secretive of them all. And that was saying something considering most of the Montgomerys always had a thing or two they kept to themselves.

When Madison looked up at him and pressed a piece of cheese to his lips, all thoughts of everybody else fled from his mind.

This was the woman he loved. The one he was going to spend the rest of his life with.

He hadn't been looking for her, but he had claimed her, nonetheless.

As he pushed her hand away slightly to capture her lips, he knew that she had claimed him just the same.

His fiancée-turned-girlfriend was the best thing that had ever happened to him.

And as his friends and family surrounded him, everybody cheering the kiss, he knew that this was only the beginning. They had many more years of this to savor, many more connections and memories to make.

But first, tonight was about family, love, their future.

And, of course, cheese.

Next in the Montgomery Ink series?

Annabelle finds her match INKED PERSUASION.

And as a bonus, Ronin, Julia, and Kincaid take a chance in CAPTURED IN INK.

WANT TO READ A SPECIAL BONUS EPILOGUE FEATURING AARON AND MADISON CLICK HERE!

A NOTE FROM CARRIE ANN RYAN

Thank you so much for reading **SEDUCED IN INK!**

I loved writing a fake-engagement romance!

Next up in the Montgomery Ink series?

Annabelle Montgomery finds her match in INKED PERSUASION. Yes, the Fort Collins Montgomerys are next!

And as a bonus, Ronin, Julia, and Kincaid take a chance in CAPTURED IN INK.

The Montgomery Ink: Boulder Series:

Book 1: Wrapped in Ink

Book 2: Sated in Ink

Book 3: Embraced in Ink

Book 3: Moments in Ink

Book 4: Seduced in Ink

Book 4.5: Captured in Ink

Book 4.7: Inked Fantasy

Book 4.8: A Very Montgomery Christmas

WANT TO READ A SPECIAL BONUS EPILOGUE FEATURING AARON AND MADISON CLICK HERE!

If you want to make sure you know what's coming next from me, you can sign up for my newsletter at www.CarrieAnnRyan.com; follow me on twitter at @CarrieAnnRyan, or like my Facebook page. I also have a Facebook Fan Club where we have trivia, chats, and other goodies. You guys are the reason I get to do what I do and I thank you.

Make sure you're signed up for my MAILING LIST so you can know when the next releases are available as well as find giveaways and FREE READS.

Happy Reading!

ALSO FROM
CARRIE ANN RYAN

The Montgomery Ink Legacy Series:

Book 1: Bittersweet Promises (Leif & Brooke)

Book 2: At First Meet (Nick & Lake)

Book 2.5: Happily Ever Never (May & Leo)

Book 3: Longtime Crush (Sebastian & Raven)

Book 4: Best Friend Temptation (Noah, Ford, and Greer)

Book 4.5: Happily Ever Maybe (Jennifer & Gus)

Book 5: Last First Kiss (Daisy & Hugh)

Book 6: His Second Chance (Kane & Phoebe)

Book 7: One Night with You (Kingston & Claire)

Book 8: Accidentally Forever (Crew & Aria)

Book 9: Last Chance Seduction (Lexington & Mercy)

Book 10: Kiss Me Forever (Brooklyn & Reece)

Book 11: His Guilty Pleasure (Dash & Aly)

Book 12: Maybe it's You (Riley & Gage)

The Cage Family

Book 1: The Forever Rule (Aston & Blakely)

Book 2: An Unexpected Everything (Isabella & Weston)

Book 3: If You Were Mine (Dorian & Harper)

Book 4: One Quick Obsession (Hudson & Scarlett)

Book 5: Pretend it's Forever (Sophia & Carson)

Book 6: Wish it Were You (Flynn & Luna)

Ashford Creek

Book 1: Legacy (Callum & Felicity)

Book 2: Crossroads (Bodhi & Kiera)

Book 3: Westward (Atlas & Elizabeth)

Book 4: Patience (Teagan & Rush)

Clover Lake

Book 1: Always a Fake Bridesmaid (Livvy & Ewan)

Book 2: Accidental Runaway Groom (Jamie & Sharp)

Book 3: His Practically Fake Proposal (Galen & Addy)

The Wilder Brothers Series:

Book 1: One Way Back to Me (Eli & Alexis)

Book 2: Always the One for Me (Evan & Kendall)

Book 3: The Path to You (Everett & Bethany)

Book 4: Coming Home for Us (Elijah & Maddie)

Book 5: Stay Here With Me (East & Lark)

Book 6: Finding the Road to Us (Elliot, Trace, and Sidney)

Book 7: Moments for You (Ridge & Aurora)

Book 7.5: A Wilder Wedding (Amos & Naomi)

Book 8: Forever For Us (Wyatt & Ava)

Book 9: Pieces of Me (Gabriel & Briar)

Book 10: Endlessly Yours (Brooks & Rory)

The Falling for the Cassidy Brothers Series:

(Formerly the First Time Series)

Book 1: Good Time Boyfriend (Heath & Devney)

Book 2: Last Minute Fiancé (Luca & Addison)

Book 3: Second Chance Husband (August & Paisley)

Montgomery Ink Denver:

Book 0.5: Ink Inspired (Shep & Shea)

Book 0.6: Ink Reunited (Sassy, Rare, and Ian)

Book 1: Delicate Ink (Austin & Sierra)

Book 1.5: Forever Ink (Callie & Morgan)

Book 2: Tempting Boundaries (Decker and Miranda)

Book 3: Harder than Words (Meghan & Luc)

Book 3.5: <u>Finally Found You</u> (Mason & Presley)

Book 4: <u>Written in Ink</u> (Griffin & Autumn)

Book 4.5: <u>Hidden Ink</u> (Hailey & Sloane)

Book 5: <u>Ink Enduring</u> (Maya, Jake, and Border)

Book 6: <u>Ink Exposed</u> (Alex & Tabby)

Book 6.5: <u>Adoring Ink</u> (Holly & Brody)

Book 6.6: <u>Love, Honor, & Ink</u> (Arianna & Harper)

Book 7: <u>Inked Expressions</u> (Storm & Everly)

Book 7.3: <u>Dropout</u> (Grayson & Kate)

Book 7.5: <u>Executive Ink</u> (Jax & Ashlynn)

Book 8: <u>Inked Memories</u> (Wes & Jillian)

Book 8.5: <u>Inked Nights</u> (Derek & Olivia)

Book 8.7: <u>Second Chance Ink</u> (Brandon & Lauren)

Book 8.5: Montgomery Midnight Kisses (Alex & Tabby Bonus(

Bonus: Inked Kingdom (Stone & Sarina)

Montgomery Ink: Colorado Springs

Book 1: Fallen Ink (Adrienne & Mace)

Book 2: Restless Ink (Thea & Dimitri)

Book 2.5: Ashes to Ink (Abby & Ryan)

Book 3: Jagged Ink (Roxie & Carter)

Book 3.5: Ink by Numbers (Landon & Kaylee)

The Montgomery Ink: Boulder Series:

Book 1: Wrapped in Ink (Liam & Arden)

Book 2: Sated in Ink (Ethan, Lincoln, and Holland)

Book 3: Embraced in Ink (Bristol & Marcus)

Book 3: Moments in Ink (Zia & Meredith)

Book 4: Seduced in Ink (Aaron & Madison)

Book 4.5: Captured in Ink (Julia, Ronin, & Kincaid)

Book 4.7: Inked Fantasy (Secret ??)

Book 4.8: A Very Montgomery Christmas (The Entire Boulder Family)

The Montgomery Ink: Fort Collins Series:

Book 1: Inked Persuasion (Jacob & Annabelle)

Book 2: Inked Obsession (Beckett & Eliza)

Book 3: Inked Devotion (Benjamin & Brenna)

Book 3.5: Nothing But Ink (Clay & Riggs)

Book 4: Inked Craving (Lee & Paige)

Book 5: Inked Temptation (Archer & Killian)

The Promise Me Series:

Book 1: Forever Only Once (Cross & Hazel)

Book 2: From That Moment (Prior & Paris)

Book 3: Far From Destined (Macon & Dakota)

Book 4: From Our First (Nate & Myra)

The Whiskey and Lies Series:

Book 1: <u>Whiskey Secrets</u> (Dare & Kenzie)

Book 2: <u>Whiskey Reveals</u> (Fox & Melody)

Book 3: <u>Whiskey Undone</u> (Loch & Ainsley)

The Gallagher Brothers Series:

Book 1: <u>Love Restored</u> (Graham & Blake)

Book 2: <u>Passion Restored</u> (Owen & Liz)

Book 3: <u>Hope Restored</u> (Murphy & Tessa)

The Carr Family Series:

(Formerly the Less Than Series)

Book 1: Breathless With Her (Devin & Erin)

Book 2: Reckless With You (Tucker & Amelia)

Book 3: Shameless With Him (Caleb & Zoey)

The Fractured Connections Series:

Book 1: Breaking Without You (Cameron & Violet)

Book 2: Shouldn't Have You (Brendon & Harmony)

Book 3: Falling With You (Aiden & Sienna)

Book 4: Taken With You (Beckham & Meadow)

The Campus Roommates Series:

(Formerly the On My Own Series)

Book 0.5: My First Glance

Book 1: My One Night (Dillon & Elise)

Book 2: My Rebound (Pacey & Mackenzie)

Book 3: My Next Play (Miles & Nessa)

Book 4: My Bad Decisions (Tanner & Natalie)

The Ravenwood Coven Series:

Book 1: Dawn Unearthed

Book 2: Dusk Unveiled

Book 3: Evernight Unleashed

The Aspen Pack Series:

Book 1: Etched in Honor

Book 2: Hunted in Darkness

Book 3: Mated in Chaos

Book 4: Harbored in Silence

Book 5: Marked in Flames

The Talon Pack:

Book 1: Tattered Loyalties

Book 2: An Alpha's Choice

Book 3: Mated in Mist

Book 4: Wolf Betrayed

Book 5: Fractured Silence

Book 6: Destiny Disgraced

Book 7: Eternal Mourning

Book 8: Strength Enduring

Book 9: Forever Broken

Book 10: Mated in Darkness

Book 11: Fated in Winter

Redwood Pack Series:

Book 0.5: <u>An Alpha's Path</u>

Book 1: <u>A Taste for a Mate</u>

Book 2: <u>Trinity Bound</u>

Book 2.5: <u>A Night Away</u>

Book 3: <u>Enforcer's Redemption</u>

Book 3.5: <u>Blurred Expectations</u>

Book 3.7: <u>Forgiveness</u>

Book 4: <u>Shattered Emotions</u>

Book 5: <u>Hidden Destiny</u>

Book 5.5: <u>A Beta's Haven</u>

Book 6: <u>Fighting Fate</u>

Book 6.5: <u>Loving the Omega</u>

Book 6.7: <u>The Hunted Heart</u>

Book 7: <u>Wicked Wolf</u>

The Elements of Five Series:

Book 1: From Breath and Ruin

Book 2: From Flame and Ash

Book 3: From Spirit and Binding

Book 4: From Shadow and Silence

Dante's Circle Series:

Book 1: <u>Dust of My Wings</u>

Book 2: <u>Her Warriors' Three Wishes</u>

Book 3: <u>An Unlucky Moon</u>

Book 3.5: <u>His Choice</u>

Book 4: <u>Tangled Innocence</u>

Book 5: <u>Fierce Enchantment</u>

Book 6: <u>An Immortal's Song</u>

Book 7: <u>Prowled Darkness</u>

Book 8: Dante's Circle Reborn

Holiday, Montana Series:

Book 1: <u>Charmed Spirits</u>

Book 2: <u>Santa's Executive</u>

Book 3: <u>Finding Abigail</u>

Book 4: <u>Her Lucky Love</u>

Book 5: Dreams of Ivory

The Branded Pack Series:

(Written with Alexandra Ivy)

Book 1: <u>Stolen and Forgiven</u>

Book 2: <u>Abandoned and Unseen</u>

Book 3: <u>Buried and Shadowed</u>

ABOUT THE AUTHOR

Carrie Ann Ryan is the New York Times and USA Today bestselling author of contemporary, paranormal, and young adult romance. Her works include the Montgomery Ink, Redwood Pack, Fractured Connections, and Elements of Five series, which have sold over 3.0 million books worldwide. She started writing while in graduate school for her advanced degree in chemistry and hasn't stopped since. Carrie Ann has written over seventy-five novels and novellas with more in the works. When she's not losing herself in her emotional and action-packed worlds, she's reading as much as she can while wrangling her clowder of cats who have more followers than she does.

www.CarrieAnnRyan.com